Trouble on Wheels

Trouble on Wheels

ANN AVELING

Cover by
BERNARD LEDUC

Scholastic Canada Ltd.

To Joannie Tabacoff
and the kids at Northlea School

Scholastic Canada Ltd.
123 Newkirk Road, Richmond Hill, Ontario, Canada L4C 3G5

Scholastic Inc.
555 Broadway, New York, NY 10012, USA

Ashton Scholastic Limited
Private Bag 1, Penrose, Auckland, New Zealand

Ashton Scholastic Pty Limited
PO Box 579, Gosford, NSW 2250, Australia

Scholastic Publications Ltd.
Villiers House, Clarendon Avenue, Leamington Spa
Warwickshire CV32 5PR, UK

Canadian Cataloguing in Publication Data

Aveling, Ann, 1953-
Trouble on wheels

ISBN 0-590-74598-0

I. Title.

PS8551.V45T7 1993   jC813'.54   C93-095428-9
PZ7.A94Tr 1993

6 5 4 3 2 1   Printed in Canada   4 5 6 7 8/9

Contents

Chapter 1

A Battered Bike

Someone had left a crumpled ball of paper on my desk. I smoothed it out and read "Hunter Watson loves Aileen Goff." Since I'm Hunter Watson and I'm not the romantic type, I knew right away that I was the victim of a practical joke. But who was the joker?

I looked over at Aileen. She was flipping the pages of her English book, her black cat earrings dancing from side to side. She seemed to be hard at work. But who could read that fast? And why was she blushing? Even her ears were red.

I scanned the room to see who else was in on it. Five people caught me looking at them. Two of them frowned. Two of them grinned. My friend Jason did both.

So I went back to the note. I flipped it over. There on the other side was somebody's math quiz, written in yellow marker. Almost every answer had a red X slashed across it. Now I knew where the note had come from.

I took the piece of paper and crumpled it back up into a ball. By now the whole class was watching. As I walked to the front of the grade five classroom, only one person continued to stare at the book in front of him. I dropped the ball of paper on his desk.

"I think this is yours," I said.

Ed Grissom turned his shaggy head in my direction, but he didn't look up.

"Oh yeah?" he said.

"Yeah," I said. "You're the only person who writes in yellow marker."

Ed shrugged. Renner, the girl sitting beside him, laughed. Mrs. Tweedie was on her feet.

"Hunter, sit down please."

I returned to my desk and opened my library book. Hidden behind its pages, I considered Ed's strange behaviour. He and Jason and I were best friends. Always had been. Always would be, or so I had thought. But now he was cool. Distant. Had I offended him somehow?

I thought back to the last time I had seen him.

Ed had come over to my house on Sunday night to listen to my new CD. While I sat at my desk drafting a code we could use for sending secret messages, he jumped around on my bed playing air guitar.

"I hate Mrs. Tweedie's new seating plan," he said at the end of a number. He dropped to his knees, then bounced back onto his feet. "Renner keeps talking to me."

I shrugged.

"That's because she sits beside you," I said.

"And when she's not talking to me, she's smiling at me," Ed said, before doing a mid-air somersault that almost broke my bed in half.

I shuddered. I knew Renner Dhali was boy crazy. All the girls said so. But I never thought she'd pick on Ed.

He leaped from one end of the bed to the other, his face glowing.

"I don't mind . . . her talking to me . . . some of the time," he said in bursts as the music and his dancing picked up speed. "She's . . ."

He yelped and collapsed in a heap. I never found out what he thought about Renner. Having just done the splits with more enthusiasm than skill, Ed was incapable of speech.

We spent the rest of the evening in the usual way: listening to some of my other CDs, eating a bag of barbecue ultra-hots, and chasing off my kid brother, Thomas, who thought he was spying on us. The same old thing.

But at school on Monday, Ed looked funny. His lunch that day was strange, too: a bread sandwich — two slices of bread with bread in the middle. I deduced that the ultra-hots were causing him ultra-stomach pain. But here it was two days later and he was still acting weird.

The bell rang, bringing me back to the present.

"Class," Mrs. Tweedie shouted above the noise of scraping chairs and snatches of conversation. "Class!" I grabbed my backpack and stuffed it full of books. Mrs. Tweedie talked to herself about gym clothes while everyone charged for the door.

I stood in the doorway, waiting for Jason. He was rummaging through the notebooks and pencil stubs and old sandwich crusts in the back of his desk. He dug out a small piece of something, peered at it, rubbed it on the leg of his jeans, and then tossed it into his mouth. It could have been food. It could have been a small bit of eraser or a scrap of paper. Jason didn't care what he chewed, just as long as it wasn't a vegetable.

Ed shouldered his knapsack and, without saying a word, pushed past.

"What's with Ed?" I asked Jason as we watched Ed stomp down the hall.

"I don't know," Jason said. "He hasn't talked to me at all today."

"He won't even look at me," I said.

Aileen and her best friend Julia Chung brushed

past us in the hallway, laughing loudly. Aileen's ears had faded to their normal pink colour. Her ponytail bobbed up and down as she laughed. So did her dangling black cat earrings. For a moment, I wondered if they were laughing at me. Being a detective, however, I deduced they were laughing about something else.

* * *

Before we even got to the end of the hall, I knew there was trouble outside. I could hear voices, many voices, raised in anger. We pushed open the doors, sprinted across the pavement and elbowed our way into the middle of a clump of kids. They were clustered around a boy from my class, Davidson Pruitt, and his bike.

Davidson's bike was chained to the link fence that runs the length of the school grounds, at the end where all the grade fives leave their bikes. It was a black and green racing bike. Or it *had been* a black and green racing bike. Now the shiny paint was scratched and scarred. The back tire had been cut in so many places it hung in strips. The front tire had been sliced open.

"I can't believe it," Davidson repeated loudly. "It's a brand new bike. It cost $349.99, *plus* tax. It was the best bike in the store, and now look at it."

"Did anybody see who did it?" I asked a group of younger kids who were pushing and shoving to get closer.

There was a chorus of "no"s.

"I saw a car back up over a bike once," a kid in grade four said. "It was at a cottage and the guy didn't know the bike was there. When he found out what he'd done, he was so mad he picked the bike up and threw it in the lake. It was great."

"I know a kid who had his bike stolen when he ran into Beckers to get a freezie," one of his friends offered.

"Was any other bike damaged?" I asked. I pushed my way out of the crowd to examine the bikes leaning against the fence.

"No," Davidson said, "Just mine." He spun the dial on his combination lock. "My dad's going to kill me, you know. He only bought it for me on Saturday and now look at it."

"Maybe one of the grade sixes did it," suggested a small boy in a blue jacket. "Or a grade seven?"

"No," I said. "All the older kids are at a track meet today."

"Maybe one of the little kids did it," someone else said.

I looked at the mangled tires and shook my head. "They wouldn't be strong enough," I said.

Jason looked at me. "Who do you think did it?" he asked.

I shrugged. "I don't have enough information yet," I said. "It could be someone from our class." But how, I wondered, and when?

"Someone's going to pay for this," Davidson said through clenched teeth. "I had the best bike in the school and now it's wrecked."

As Jason and I watched, Davidson walked the wobbling bike through the school gate. His friends rode their bikes in big slow circles in the middle of the street waiting for him to catch up. A crowd of little kids tagged along.

I shook my head. It was a disturbing sight.

Chapter 2

Hunter Watson, Detective

I have quite a reputation as a detective. I've been solving cases ever since I was four. That was when I pointed out to my father that he always lost his wallet on Friday mornings because it was garbage day. His wallet used to fall out of his inner breast pocket into the garbage can as he wrestled it down to the curb. So he bought a garbage can on wheels that he doesn't have to lean over. Case closed.

I've solved a lot of mysteries since then: what happened to the kindergarten teacher's goldfish, who stole Becca daSilva's ski jacket, where the music teacher disappeared to every afternoon at 3:45 sharp. So I wasn't surprised when Davidson Pruitt phoned me that evening to ask if I'd solved this case.

"I'm still working on it," I told him.

"Don't bother," Davidson said. "My dad's going to get me a new bike with the insurance money."

I thought about telling him that we detectives don't just give up on a case. Then I thought of reminding him that I didn't need his permission to proceed.

"Listen, Davidson," I began, but it was too late. Davidson wasn't interested in anything I had to say. He was off in his own private world, talking about his favourite subject: money. "The insurance company will give him about 200 bucks, because they have to deduct the first 100 dollars, but that's okay," Davidson continued. "I'll make sure he comes up with the rest. He can put it on his American Express card."

Davidson rambled on about his father's credit cards and how much money he spent on them every month. It was amazing. Davidson was talking thousands of dollars, tens of thousands of dollars. But then again, maybe it wasn't true. I could distinctly remember him telling our grade two class that his new sneakers cost a million dollars.

Finally he ran out of breath.

"That's about it," he said. "Just thought you might be worried about the money. Bye." He hung up the phone.

That was typical Davidson Pruitt. Anyone else would be heartbroken or furious. But Davidson probably hadn't given another thought to his shattered bike. Instead he was busy spending the insurance money. I wondered if he played Monopoly in his sleep.

* * *

I arrived at school the next morning seven minutes before the bell rang. I locked my bike beside Jason's and joined the rest of the guys by the side doors. Jason, Davidson Pruitt, and a bunch of the grade fours were standing around listening to Max Goldhar, Davidson's best friend.

"There are twenty of them in the gang," Max was saying, as he tossed a fluorescent yellow tennis ball from hand to hand. "They call themselves the Death Heads and they go around bashing people over the head and stealing their leather jackets."

Jason and Davidson nodded in agreement.

"Wow!" said one of the younger kids.

"And if people don't give them what they want, they throw them in front of the subway trains," Max continued.

Jason and Davidson nodded again.

"But what if they're not in the subway?" another kid asked.

"They drag them to the nearest subway station and then they throw them in front of a train," Max said cheerfully. He tossed the tennis ball high in the air and stepped neatly underneath to catch it.

Brent Wexler ambled over to join us, the laces on his running shoes flopping from side to side, his usual half-smile in place. Brent had a very strange face. I spent a whole month last year sitting across from him in class, wondering what it was that bothered me. Finally I got it. If you looked at the right-hand side of his face, he looked serious. If you looked at the left-hand side, he had a slight grin. Put them both together and you had Brent, part silly, part sensible. But more silly than sensible.

"So, who busted Davidson's bike?" he asked me.

Everyone turned to stare.

"I'm still investigating," I said.

"I think I know who did it," he said.

"Who?" Davidson asked. He took a step forward.

"Jeremy Diskau," Brent said.

I frowned.

"Why do you say that?" I asked. Diskau was in our class. I had never heard of him getting in trouble before. Come to think of it, I'd never heard anyone even mention him. He'd been at our school for less than a year and didn't seem to have any friends.

"Because Jeremy was out of the classroom for a long time yesterday afternoon," Brent said.

He was standing to my left, so it was the serious side of his face that I saw.

"That's because Jeremy was in the nurse's

office getting medicine for his asthma," I said, testing Brent's theory.

"But he usually goes at recess," Brent said. "Not right after recess."

Brent had a point there. It was surprisingly observant of him. Maybe he was smarter than I thought.

"He wouldn't be strong enough," Jason said. "Not with asthma."

"Sure he would," Brent said. "I had asthma when I was a kid and it didn't bother me. I just coughed a lot."

"My brother has asthma," Max said as he threw the tennis ball high over our heads.

"I didn't know that!" I said. Jake Goldhar was the fastest tennis player I'd ever seen.

"He hardly ever gets it," Max said. He bumped one of the grade fours out of the way as he caught the ball. "It's only when he exercises really hard that he starts wheezing. So before a match he breathes through this puffer thing with the medicine in it and he's okay."

"Forget the asthma," Davidson said. "What you're telling me is that big fat Jeremy Diskau wrecked $349.99 worth of bike!"

"Why would he want to smash Davidson's bike?" I asked.

"Maybe he's crazy," Brent suggested. He turned to me and winked his left eye. That was typical of him. Just when I thought he was getting serious, he said something stupid again.

"He *must* be crazy if he thinks he can go around smashing other people's expensive equipment!" Davidson snorted.

"That's what you get for having such a rich bike," Brent said.

I used to feel sorry for Brent, back in the days when I listened to him moan about how poor he was. Then I saw the mega-mansion he lived in. Obviously, his parents had lots of money.

"There's Jeremy." Jason pointed.

We turned to look. Jeremy Diskau slowly wheeled an old five-speed to an empty portion of fence. He unwound the bicycle chain from the crossbar and carefully threaded it through the front wheel.

"I saw him at the swimming pool last spring when I was taking Life Saving 3," Max said, tossing the tennis ball from hand to hand. "He was floating in the shallow end."

"Maybe he was in Tiny Tots," Brent said. We all laughed. Jeremy was one of the tallest kids in the class, and certainly the heaviest.

He trudged past us toward the school doors. His round face turned in our direction, but he didn't smile or speak. Instead, he hauled one of the doors open and stepped inside.

The bell rang.

As we filed into school, Davidson hissed in my ear. "We've got to get him, Hunter."

Chapter 3

Problems, Problems

Before I even got to my desk, I could tell that Mrs. Tweedie was in a bad mood. Her mouth was set in a thin line and her jaw stuck out. As we hung up our jackets and backpacks, she beat a brisk rhythm on her desk with a pencil.

"*When* you are ready," she said, "we will begin." Most people had the sense to sit down and shut up. But Brent scuffled with Max for the same coathook.

"Brent! Max!" Mrs. Tweedie snapped. "Sit down, please."

Max gave Brent a combination elbow jab and hip check before trotting to his seat. Brent lingered by the book centre, flipping the pages of a paperback. His smiling face was turned to Mrs. Tweedie.

"Brent Wexler, you may go to the vice-principal's office and explain to her why you are incapable of responding to a simple request."

Brent looked surprised. We all did. Brent had been sent to the vice-principal's office the year before for ripping the straps off Julia's brand-new knapsack. But he'd never been sent for something as minor as this. None of us had.

"Off you go!" she said.

This time he went.

"Math books out, please," she said.

Twenty-two math books appeared on twenty-three desks. Max, who sat opposite me, stuffed the tennis ball away in his desk and got out his dictionary. He caught me looking at him and rolled his eyes. I deduced that he had forgotten his math book at home and hoped to avoid detection. I didn't think he stood a chance.

Jeremy Diskau walked into the room and went to the back to hang up his jacket.

"Where is your late slip?" Mrs. Tweedie demanded.

"I was in the nurse's office," Jeremy replied.

"I need a late slip," she said slowly and distinctly. "You go and get a late slip."

He turned and left. No one spoke. No one whispered. It looked to me as if Max had forgotten how to breathe.

"We will start with yesterday's lesson, page

thirty-seven," she said. "Does anyone need a review?"

The only sound was of twenty-two math books being opened to page thirty-seven and one dictionary being opened to the letter D.

"Very well, since you all understand these concepts, we will move on to page thirty-eight. Julia, would you please do the first problem."

Julia Chung stumbled through the first problem. Mrs. Tweedie listened to her in complete silence and didn't ask anyone to help her out. We usually work on these exercises in teams. Mrs. Tweedie seemed to have lost her team spirit.

When Julia finished, Mrs. Tweedie merely nodded and said "Ed?"

"What?" Ed asked. His shoulders were hunched so high I could barely see his head above his red sweatshirt.

"Will you do the second problem?" Mrs. Tweedie said.

I groaned. There was no way in the world that Ed would be able to do this unassisted.

"Are you feeling ill, Hunter?" Mrs. Tweedie glared at me.

"Not yet," I said politely, as I watched Jeremy Diskau slip back into the room and hand Mrs. Tweedie a note before hanging up his jacket. Davidson snarled at him as he went by. Mrs. Tweedie yanked my attention back.

"Then *you* may do the second problem," she said.

I had got Ed off the hook all right. I hoped my problems weren't just beginning. I examined the second question.

"It looks pretty straightforward to me," I said.

"I didn't ask you to describe it," she said. "I asked you to solve it."

Solving problems is my life's work. This one was no tougher than many others I had met. I squinted my eyes, did a few quick calculations and gave her the right answer. She looked disappointed.

Brent shuffled through the door, bumped into the back of Davidson's chair and stumbled to his desk. Mrs. Tweedie scowled at him.

"We're on page thirty-eight," she said. She surveyed the class. Max had sunk way down in his chair. I thought it was poor strategy on his part. So did Mrs. Tweedie.

"Max," she said. "You may do the third problem." Max's face went white, then red, then white again.

Renner Dhali suddenly gasped and grabbed Ed's arm.

"Renner!" Mrs. Tweedie snapped.

"But there's a spider, Mrs. Tweedie," Renner shrieked, her eyes fixed on a point above Mrs. Tweedie. "Right over your head!"

Mrs. Tweedie brushed a hand over the top of her hair, moaned, put her other hand to her mouth and ran out of the room. We clustered around the spot where she'd been standing. Sure enough, a large, furry spider lay on its back on the carpet. Three of its legs were waving. The other five had curled up.

"Kill it, Ed," Renner pleaded.

"Don't be an idiot," Bretta Haanapel said firmly. "Does anyone have a jar I can put it in?"

Aileen Goff donated the margarine tub she brought olives in for lunch.

"You can have this," she said, after dumping the olives into her hand. "Just as long as that spider doesn't come near me."

"Or me," Renner said.

"I'll keep in it my desk," Bretta promised. She got to work poking holes in the lid with a sharp pencil.

Mrs. Tweedie reappeared looking pale and serious. "I think we'll go on to the three-dimensional shapes we started last week," she said. "Please get into your groups."

Max stuffed his dictionary into his desk. He was grinning so hard I was surprised his face didn't crack. He vaulted over his chair and went to join his group.

Aileen and Julia came over to join Jason and me. Aileen still cradled a handful of shiny olives.

She glanced around to see that Mrs. Tweedie wasn't looking, then offered them to us. We shook our heads. She popped them in her mouth.

Julia pulled her hairband off and shook her thick, black hair around. Then she slid the hairband on again. Her hair didn't look any different for all that shaking. What was the point?

"Can you help me get the straws and stuff?" she said to Jason. They went to the back closet to get the supplies.

I lifted our three-dimensional shape down from the window ledge. It was a pyramid made up of different kinds of triangles. We'd reinforced the row of triangles around the base by using two straws for each triangle side instead of one. We were on our fourth level now and our structure was almost wobble-free.

Aileen swallowed the last of the olives. She rubbed her wet hands on her jeans and said, "I bet Mrs. Tweedie had a fight with her husband this morning."

"Maybe," I said, as I checked the corner of the pyramid that was slightly askew.

"She probably didn't pick up his shirts from the dry cleaner's," Aileen said. "My parents always have fights about stuff like that."

"Maybe," I said.

"What do you think?" she persisted.

"I think we need to reinforce this corner," I said.

"No, about Mrs. Tweedie. Hunter, you're not paying attention. What do you think about Mrs. Tweedie?"

"I think she's in a rotten mood today," I said. What more did Aileen want?

Jason and Julia returned with the supply bin.

"We need some more string to hold this together," I said, pointing to the bulging corner.

"This much?" Jason asked, as he unreeled a length of green string.

"Great," I said.

He cut off a length of string for me and an equal length for himself. Julia frowned at him as he stuffed it in his mouth.

"Maybe she had a flat tire on the way to school," Aileen continued.

"Who?" Julia asked.

"Mrs. Tweedie," Aileen explained. "First she had a terrible fight with her husband and then she got a flat tire on the way to school."

"She did?" Julia asked.

"No wonder she's in such a terrible mood," Jason said.

"No, no, no," I said. "This is Aileen's idea. We don't know why Mrs. Tweedie's so mad."

"My mother was really mad at my dad yesterday," Jason said. "He said something about the laundry never getting done and she went crazy."

"And the shirts not coming back from the dry

cleaner's on time," Aileen said and nodded her head.

Mrs. Tweedie's voice came from over my right shoulder. "And how are we coming along?" she said coldly.

There was a moment's silence. The back of my neck prickled.

"Okay," I said.

"You don't seem to be making any progress," she said.

"We're just reinforcing the base before we build it any higher," I said.

Julia and Aileen nodded in agreement.

"Remember your ratios. And less talking and more working," she said and turned to Ed's group. I noticed that Ed wasn't there.

"I hope Mrs. Tweedie remembers to pick up the shirts after school today," Aileen said and sighed. I found myself agreeing with her. Jason discovered my ruler in his desk and we got to work measuring the straws.

Chapter 4

Another Attack

For the next forty-five minutes, we worked on our shapes. Mrs. Tweedie sat at her desk going through a stack of papers. I kept an eye on her, just in case she decided to blow up again. But she was quiet now.

The recess bell rang. Jason and I were the last to leave. Jason was sure he had an extra sweet-and-sour stick hidden in the back of his desk. I was leaning in the doorway waiting for him to give up when Davidson Pruitt burst through the far doors.

"Hunter, hey Hunter," he called.

Halfway down the hall, Mr. Feeney stuck his head out of the grade eight classroom.

"No shouting in the halls," he shouted at

Davidson. He turned to me. "You're supposed to be outside," he yelled.

I grabbed Jason and we went to see what Davidson wanted.

* * *

Another bike had been attacked, this one more viciously than the first. Not only were the tires slashed into limp shreds and the paint scratched, but this time the bicycle chain had been wrenched off.

Max touched his ruined bike with one trembling finger, his eyes wet. His fluorescent yellow tennis ball dropped from his hand and rolled to rest by the slivered front tire.

"Okay, who did it?" Davidson roared at the crowd, his face an angry red.

There was a wave of shrugs and a chorus of "not me"s. I didn't think much of his approach. Did he really think anyone was going to admit it, just like that? He needed an expert's help.

"Who was the first one here?" I shouted over the noise.

"We were," some little boys announced. "Our class was the first class out."

"What did you see?" I asked them.

"Nothing," they said. "We wanted to get to the climber first, so we never looked that way."

That made sense. The climber was about twenty metres away from the bike.

"Who was here next?"

About ten kids said they were. I spoke to each of them individually. No one had seen anything out of the ordinary, but all of them had seen the battered bike. Or so they said.

"Stand back, everyone," I ordered. "I want to examine the scene of the crime."

The kids at the front of the crowd took a step back. The kids at the back of the crowd took a step forward to see what was going on. There was a lot of pushing and shoving where they met.

I turned my back on the mob and concentrated on the bike.

The damage had been done by someone with a knife. A sharp knife. The front tire had been cut in three places. The back tire was cut in seventeen places. The chain was hanging loose. To the trained eye, it looked like someone had grabbed it and yanked it. Hard.

This could be my lucky break, I thought. The chain was black with axle grease. That meant that even the untrained eye should be able to identify the culprit by his black, greasy hands.

I stood up and addressed the crowd. "Let me see your hands," I said.

"Why?" someone asked.

"I want to see your hands. Whoever did this should have black grease on their hands."

I watched closely as everyone stuck their hands

out. No one wiped their hands on their clothes first or stuck them in their pockets. Did this mean the guilty person wasn't here?

I walked through the crowd, examining each pair separately. What I discovered was very interesting. Nobody's hands were clean. Some hands were speckled with different coloured marker ink. Some had been drawn on in pen. I tried not to think about what could have caused some of the other strange splotches I saw. By the time I had examined thirty-six pairs of hands, I felt compelled to examine my own. I had dirt under the fourth fingernail on my right hand.

Fascinating as this was from a scientific point of view, it didn't get me any closer to solving the crime.

"Why wouldn't the person just wash his hands?" Aileen Goff objected. "Or hers, I guess." Aileen's fingers rested in mine for a moment. They were soft and almost clean. I didn't like the green nail polish, though.

"This is industrial grease. It's heavy. It would take a lot of washing to get rid of it all. And a lot of soap."

"But someone could go to the washroom and scrub it off," Aileen insisted.

"Why don't you check the girls' washrooms and see if there's any evidence of someone scrubbing black grease from their hands," I said. "I'll check the boys'. We'll discuss it at lunch."

"Okay," she said.

"Where's Jeremy Diskau?" Jason asked.

"Good question," I said. I surveyed the schoolyard, looking for his round, pale face. The crowd was thinning out. Kids drifted off for a few minutes of play before recess ended. I couldn't see Jeremy anywhere.

"Why do you want to know?" Aileen asked.

"A theory we have," I said, with a wave of my hand.

"He could have done it because he's always out of the classroom," Jason explained. "He could say he's going to the nurse's office and then he could sneak outside when no one's looking and smash up someone's bike."

"Wow!" Aileen and Julia said, their eyes wide and fixed on Jason.

"Of course it's only an idea," I said.

They ignored me.

"So when he came in late this morning, he'd been outside wrecking Max's bike," Julia said. She held her headband, forgetting for a moment to go through the hair-tossing routine.

Aileen shook her head from side to side. Her black cat earrings danced furiously.

"That's awful," she said. "What a mean thing to do."

"We don't know it was Jeremy," I objected. "It's

just a theory. It could be anyone who left the room this morning. What about Brent? He got sent up to the office. And people were in and out going to the washroom all morning."

I had an idea that someone else had been absent during the crucial time, but I couldn't remember who. And what about the axle grease? It was becoming quite a mystery. The bell rang.

Chapter 5

Searching for Clues

When Mrs. Tweedie sent Max to the office to report the crime, Davidson glared at Jeremy. So did the other boys. Jeremy sat, his head down, not looking at anyone in the room. Was this the way a guilty person would behave? Max returned and there was a rush of conversation.

"Don't worry, the insurance company . . . " "Are you okay, Max? . . . " "Do you want a brownie at lunch? . . . " "Max, I have your book for you . . . "

"Quiet, please," Mrs. Tweedie said. "I'd like to — "

She was interrupted by an announcement on the intercom. It was the principal, Mrs. Boswell, telling us that vandalism on school property would not be tolerated and asking anyone with information to come up to the office to see her. No one left the room.

"We will continue with our haikus," Mrs. Tweedie said. "I'd like to hear what you've been working on." Everyone got to read a verse. Some were funny, some were strange. I noticed Mrs. Tweedie shivered when Brent read his:

one-eyed cat
five-legged spider
blood and guts on the floor

He must have re-written it to get in that part about the spider. There was a brief discussion about whether or not spiders bleed. Mrs. Tweedie cut the conversation short and told us to continue our reading assignments.

* * *

When the lunch bell rang, I joined the kids surging out of the school on their way home. But I wasn't going home for lunch. I was checking the bikes.

"They're all okay," a grade three kid told me as he unlocked his chain and wheeled his bike out. "Except that one," pointing to Max's mangled bike.

I nodded, then went back into the school, down to the lunchroom. I saw Jeremy sitting alone at the far table. Aileen grabbed me on my way past.

"I checked all the girls' washrooms," she said. "There's no black grease in any of them, although one of the classes in the primary wing must be finger-painting. There's yellow and orange blobs on everything."

I admired her scientific enthusiasm.

"Good work," I said. Then I had an idea. "We're going to go out and look for clues. Why don't you keep your eye on Jeremy? Find out what he's up to."

"Sure," she said, her black cat earrings bobbing as she turned in his direction.

I sat down with the guys.

"Eat fast," I told them. "We'll go out and search for clues as soon as lunch is over."

Davidson stuffed half a sandwich in his mouth and threw the other half over the table into the garbage can.

"I'm ready," he said.

Max put an apple back in his lunchbox and closed the lid.

"Me too," he said.

I opened my lunchbox and examined its contents. My mother had packed another nutritious meal. I helped myself to a handful of Jason's nachos and emptied my lunchbox into the garbage can.

The clock on the lunchroom wall read 12:20.

"Time to go," I said.

We all stood up. All but Ed. He stayed in his seat, scooping handfuls of breakfast cereal out of a bag and dribbling them into his open mouth.

"I'll be there later," he sputtered.

"Okay," I said, eyeing the cereal. Then I got down to business. "We'll examine the school grounds for evidence," I said. "We'll go over every square centimetre, starting with the area closest to the bikes. There's got to be a clue somewhere."

Davidson, Max and Jason twisted their way between the chairs and tables and garbage cans to the double doors. I cruised the tables on the way, telling people what was going on. I found myself at my little brother Thomas's table.

"I've got a job for you guys," I said.

The grade one kids jumped up and down. All except my brother.

"What is it?" Thomas asked suspiciously.

"I need some sharp eyes to search the schoolyard for clues," I said. "We've got to find out who's smashing bikes."

"I'll help!" Derek said. He was Thomas' best friend. I grabbed two of his cookies to hurry him along.

Thomas frowned.

"Don't take all Derek's cookies," he said. "Derek, tell him to stop. Hunter, stop! Don't eat all his cookies."

"I don't mind," Derek said. "Here, Hunter." He gave me a third cookie.

I could hear Thomas muttering to himself. "My

friend . . . should be my cookies," it sounded like. I knew the feeling. Our mother was nutrition-crazy. If I could make her pack a normal lunch, we wouldn't have to go begging.

I made a mental note to investigate the matter further. But first, I had a job to do.

"I want you guys to look everywhere," I said. "If you find anything suspicious, bring it to me."

They charged out of the lunchroom in a pack. Thomas sat scowling in his seat for a moment, then ran after them. I finished Derek's Coke and followed.

Chapter 6

A Witness Appears

"Hunter, over here!" Jason called from across the playground. I jogged over to where he stood with Max, Davidson and a small boy in a huge jean jacket. The kid's jacket hung down to his knees and the cuffs had been rolled back two or three times.

"This kid actually saw it," Jason said.

"My bike. He saw the guy who busted my bike," Max said.

"Now we'll get him," Davidson said. "We'll really make him pay."

"Okay, okay," I said. I turned to the kid. "Tell me what you saw."

"A big boy in a red jacket," he squeaked.

"Start at the beginning," I said. "Tell me everything."

He looked from me to Jason and back again.

"Well," he said, "for breakfast I had honey-nut flakes and toast and honey and pop-up waffles and honey and a bowl of oatmeal." He thought for a moment. "With brown sugar," he added.

I looked him in amazement. No wonder his mother bought him such big clothes. He was starting out small, but if he ate all that for breakfast every morning, he wouldn't stay small for long.

He continued.

"Then I watched some television and my mother told me it was library day and I didn't know where my book was and then . . . "

I interrupted. I wanted the facts of the case, not the story of his life.

"When did you see someone in a red jacket attack the bike?" I asked.

"When we were running laps for gym," he answered.

I nodded. The kindergarten kids often ran laps around the playground area during their gym period. As they rounded the south-west corner of the field, they'd be able to see the fence where Max had locked his bike.

"What time was that?" I asked.

"I don't know," he said.

"You didn't look at your watch?" I said, pointing to the heavy, black, water-proof, pressure-proof, scratch-resistant watch on his wrist.

He looked at me with surprise.

"No," he said. "I can't tell time yet."

I tried to hide my frustration.

"Do you have any idea what time it was?" I asked. "Was it before recess?"

"Yes," he said. "But not just before recess, earlier than that."

"Was it right after attendance?" I asked.

"No," he said slowly. "We have show and tell after attendance."

"Was it after show and tell?" I tried again.

He grinned. His bottom two teeth were missing.

"Yes," he said. "That's when it was."

"Good," I said. Progress was slow, but steady. "What did you see?"

"A big boy in a red jacket," the kid answered. "I saw him run over and grab a bike."

"And then what did you see?" I asked.

"Nothing," he said. "Mason Dee started to catch up and I wanted to beat him, so I didn't look any more."

"What did he look like?"

"He's bigger than me but I can run faster and he has a Blue Jays jacket and . . . "

"Wait a minute," I said. "I thought you said he had a red jacket."

"The big boy had a red jacket," the kid said.

"Isn't that who we're talking about?" I asked.

"I'm talking about Mason Dee," the kid said.

I sighed.

"Let's talk about the big boy," I said slowly and clearly. "What did the big boy look like?"

"I don't know," the kid said. "He was just big, that's all."

"Was he as tall as I am?" I asked.

"I don't know," he replied. "I wasn't really looking. I was watching for Mason Dee and I saw the big boy in the red jacket. But I didn't stare at him because Mason Dee was catching up."

"We'll do an instant replay," I said. I looked around at my circle of friends. From the school doors, Ed wandered over to where we stood. He was one of the tallest people in the class.

"Ed," I said when he reached us, "I want you to go to the far doors and when I give the signal, run over to where Max's bike is and pretend to stab it."

Ed looked alarmed.

"No way," he said.

"We're just recreating the crime," I explained. "This kid here . . . "

"Jonathan," the small boy interrupted.

"Jonathan witnessed the event, although it's too bad he didn't pay more attention." I gave Jonathan a stern look before turning back to Ed. "So we want you to pretend to be the attacker and Jonathan can tell us whether the guy was about the same size as you."

"No way," said Ed.

"Why not?" I said. What was Ed's problem anyway? I'd have to have a serious talk with him. And soon.

"I just don't want to," he said. He turned and walked slowly back the way he'd come. We watched him go in silence.

"I'll do it," Jason said. "I'm average height. It'll give you an idea about how tall this guy really is."

Jason loped off toward the doors of the school. I got Jonathan into position, then waved at Jason. He leaped out of the doorway, dashed the fifteen metres and lunged at the fence. It was a very athletic performance.

"What do you think?" I asked Jonathan.

He shrugged.

"I don't know," he said. He frowned. "I guess that's what he looked like. But he didn't jump around like that. I don't know." His frown deepened.

"But he was wearing a red jacket?" I asked, hoping my one clue wasn't going to disappear.

"Yeah," Jonathan said. He looked happier. "He was wearing a red jacket."

A gang of little kids on the climber waved at us. Jonathan waved back.

"Can I go now?" he asked.

"Sure," I said. "If I have any further questions, I'll let you know. And if you remember anything, or if any of your friends saw anything, you come find me, okay?"

"Okay," he said cheerfully. He ran off to join his friends.

"What do you think?" Jason asked.

"He's sure about the red jacket," I said. "But that's about all."

"Jeremy has a red jacket," Jason said to me quietly.

"I know," I said.

"And he's the biggest kid in the class," Jason said.

"That's right," I said.

"So we've got our proof," Jason said. "What'll we do now? Do you want to phone the police? Or go see the principal?"

"I'm not convinced," I said slowly, reluctantly.

"What more do you want?" Jason asked.

I couldn't answer him. I didn't know. But something told me that the case wasn't over yet. I'd noticed something, or maybe someone had told me something, that made me doubt Jeremy's guilt. Too bad I couldn't remember what it was. Well, it would come back to me. I was sure of it.

Derek and Thomas rushed over to where we stood. Derek held a brick in his hand.

"Look what I found," he said proudly.

"That's nice," I said politely.

"It's a clue," Thomas told me. He grabbed the

brick. "We found it over by the fence. We bet it was used to smash that bike."

I took it from him.

"Hey, you didn't say please," Thomas complained.

"Don't be ridiculous," I said to him. I showed the brick to Jason.

"I don't know," Jason said. "Max's bike wasn't bashed in, it was cut."

"Sliced," I agreed. "Sorry kids," I said to Thomas and Derek. "I don't think this is the murder weapon."

Derek groaned. Thomas raged.

"It is too! You're just saying that, Hunter, because you don't want us to have any fun! You want to keep it all for yourself . . . "

Brent Wexler skidded to a stop beside me, almost tripping over the laces of his running shoes. He held out a gym shirt, stained across the chest with black grease.

"Look at this," he said in short, sharp breaths. "I found, I found, I found . . . " He took one deep breath and let it out slowly. "I found it stuffed in the garbage can by the side doors."

"Good work!" I said as I inspected the shirt. The print of a bicycle chain was visible in the mess. Now I knew how the slasher had escaped detection. He'd wrapped the gym shirt around his hand before grabbing the chain. It was a clever trick.

"I bet it's Jeremy's shirt," Brent said in a hoarse voice. He cleared his throat.

"Check the label," Jason said.

Everyone was supposed to have their name written on their T-shirt since it was part of the gym uniform. The label read: "Penman's. Made in Canada. Size: L." That was it.

"There's no name!" Jason wailed.

"Bet Jeremy isn't in uniform next gym day," Brent said, between coughs.

The bell rang.

* * *

I kept a careful watch on Jeremy that afternoon. He was as quiet as ever. I wished I'd noticed him more before the bicycle slasher struck. Was this his normal behaviour?

While I was wondering, Aileen strolled by my desk and dropped a crumpled ball of paper on it. Another note. I was surprised and a little worried. I hoped it wasn't about me or her or some kind of "us." I smoothed out the paper.

"Dear Hunter," the note said. "Jeremy ate 2 sandwiches (ham, I think), a can of C-plus and a bunch of crackers for lunch. He also ate an apple!!! Weird!!! The lunchroom monitors made him go outside after lunch, but he just stood by the doors for a while and then went back in!!!!!" It was signed "Aileen." Over the "i" was a heart. I hoped it had no special meaning.

There was a P.S.: "Julia saw Jeremy kick a dog once. It was a poodle."

I looked up from the note to see Aileen watching me. I nodded my thanks. For some reason, she blushed. I decided not to figure out what this meant and instead devoted myself to an investigation of my science project.

Chapter 7

What's the Matter with Ed?

After school I called an emergency meeting of my detectives. Jason, Ed and I met in my bedroom.

"We've got to get Jeremy before he wrecks someone else's bike," Jason insisted.

"I'm still not sure it's him," I said.

Jason groaned.

Ed slumped on the corner of my bed. He'd hardly spoken since we got home. The only time he looked happy was when he was eating a triple-decker peanut butter, jam and peanut butter sandwich, washed down with a litre of milk. Blobs of jam splattered the front of his red sweatshirt.

"What do you think?" I asked him.

"About what?" he said.

I stared at him.

"Are you okay?" I asked.

"Me?" he said. "I'm great." He bared his teeth in what was supposed to be a smile. I wasn't fooled.

"You guys are crazy," Jason shouted. He jumped off the bed, stalked over to my desk, ripped off a strip of paper and stuffed it in his mouth. He jumped back onto the bed, chewing loudly.

"We've got all the evidence we need," he said. "I think we should do something about it. Not wait for someone else's bike to get blasted."

"Who says more bikes are going to get smashed?" I asked.

"The guy's obviously crazy," Jason explained. "Renner said she heard Jeremy talking about all the drugs he takes for his asthma. You know what drugs can do to you!"

"I've got to go," Ed said. He hauled himself to his feet.

"Wait a minute," I said. "What's the matter? Why are you going?"

But I was too late. One minute he was slouched on the bed, his eyes half-closed. The next, he was on his feet, running for the door.

"I've got to go," he repeated as he yanked the door open. Thomas fell into the room. Ed stepped over him and thundered down the stairs.

"I didn't mean to. I wasn't listening," Thomas whined. I pushed my way past him, but Ed was gone. I returned to my room. Jason was sitting on top of Thomas.

"You're hurting me, you're hurting me," Thomas was moaning.

"You know what we do with spies," I said between clenched teeth.

"Mom!" he yelled, "Mom! Hunter's hurting me."

"You think *this* is pain," I said.

"Anyway, I wasn't spying," he said quickly. "I came to tell you something."

"And that's why you were kneeling by the door," I said sarcastically.

"Tell us another one," Jason added.

"I can tell you one thing," Thomas said. "The gym shirt came from the Lost and Found."

Jason rolled off Thomas and stood up. Thomas unbent himself, groaning loudly. If he thought we'd feel sorry for him, he was wrong. He wasn't a very good actor. It remained to be seen how good a detective he was.

"How do you know?" I asked.

"Because I saw it there this morning," Thomas said

"What were you doing at the Lost and Found?" I asked.

"Nothing much. Just checking it out," he said. "You know," he added.

I did know. Thomas looked on the Lost and Found as his own territory. If something stayed there for more than a day or two, he decided it was public property. If he liked it, he picked it up and brought it home. He called it recycling. I called it theft.

"How do you know it was the same shirt?" I asked.

"The sleeve was ripped," he said. I looked surprised. "Ha! Ha! You didn't know that, did you? Ha! Ha!"

"Of course I knew the sleeve was ripped," I said with an air of quiet dignity. "I had not yet determined whether it was ripped during the commission of the crime or before it."

"What?" Thomas looked puzzled.

"Off you go," I said, pushing him out of the room. "Don't come spying on us again or you'll really be in trouble."

"Wait! You guys! No!" he said, but it was useless. I shoved him into the hallway and closed my door again.

"Some people never say thank you," I heard him say. I motioned for silence until we heard his footsteps thumping down the stairs.

"He really was listening," Jason said.

"He's a pest," I agreed. "But what do you think of this new evidence?"

"It doesn't seem to help much," he shrugged.

"It could be anyone's shirt." I frowned. We needed more facts.

Jason frowned too.

"What's the matter with Ed?" he asked.

I shook my head.

"I don't know," I said. "One minute we're talking about Jeremy taking drugs and the next minute Ed's gone." A terrible thought occurred to me. "You don't think Ed's taking drugs, do you?"

"No way," Jason said immediately. "His brother would kill him."

Jason was right. A few years ago, when Simon started high school, he got in with a wild gang of older kids and was been picked up by the cops on a drug charge. The judge had given him a suspended sentence, but he knew he wouldn't get off so easy next time. Nobody was tougher on drugs now than Simon.

"I don't understand it," I said. "We're talking about Jeremy taking drugs for his asthma, which Renner says she heard about . . . "

"That's it," Jason interrupted me, his voice cracking. "It's Renner! Hunter, I'm afraid Ed is in love."

It was one explanation, all right. But could it be the right one?

Chapter 8

Davidson's Justice

The next morning the sky was a clear, bright blue. I left my jacket in the classroom at recess and strolled out into the warm sunshine to find Aileen's bike battered and slashed. The tires were shredded. The chain hung tangled from the left pedal.

"My bike!" she screeched when she saw it. She clapped a hand over her mouth and swayed back and forth.

Julia ran to her side.

"That's it," Davidson Pruitt roared. "I'm going to kill him."

No one needed to ask who he was talking about. Instead a wave of voices said "Yeah," and "Go get him."

"Me too," Max said through clenched teeth. His hands tightened into fists.

Aileen shrugged off Julia's arm.

"I'm going to tell the principal all about this," she said.

Julia nodded her head violently, her black hair flying. "She'll phone the police and they can arrest him," she agreed.

"I'm going to pound him first," Davidson said.

"Me too!" Max said. He raced off around the corner of the school at the head of a gang of boys.

Aileen and Julia led the girls up the wide front steps of the school to the principal's office.

Jason and I stayed where we were. I crouched by the mangled bike and examined it, centimetre by centimetre. This attack looked just like the others.

Brent wandered over to join us, his hands in his jacket pocket, his shoe laces flopping.

"What did I tell you?" he said. "Another expensive bike trashed. That Diskau is one crazy kid."

"Maybe," I said.

"What about fingerprints?" he asked. "Do you think there are any fingerprints on the bike?"

"I doubt it," I said. "I think that's one of the reasons this guy used a gym shirt on Max's bike. So he wouldn't leave prints. He probably did the same thing for this bike too."

"It sure is sad to see a beautiful bike ruined,"

he continued. Typical Brent, I thought as I looked up at him. He was smiling as he said it. "If this keeps up, soon people won't want to bring their brand-new bikes to school. Everyone'll be riding old garbage bikes like mine." His laughter sounded bitter. "Have you seen Ed anywhere?" he changed the subject abruptly.

"No, why?" I asked.

"Just wondering," he said. "Ed doesn't seem to be around much anymore."

Before I had a chance to wonder what he meant, the guys were back, dragging Jeremy. Davidson and Max each held one of his arms. A pack of younger kids followed, shouting encouragement and insults.

The front doors of the school flew open and I saw Aileen, Julia and the girls from my class lead the principal toward us. Brent, I noticed, faded into the background.

Jeremy looked terrified. He was turning from Davidson to Max and back again.

"Let go," he said in a rough voice. "I didn't do anything. I don't know what you're talking about."

"Davidson Pruitt! Max Goldhar! Stop that right now," the principal called.

Max dropped Jeremy's arm. I saw Davidson pinch it as he let go.

Mrs. Boswell marched over to where we stood.

"This kind of violent behaviour is completely

inappropriate," she said in a high, clear voice. "Max, Davidson and Jeremy, come with me."

One of the new teachers at the school suddenly appeared around the far side of the building. Mrs. Boswell gave her a cold look.

"Ms Babiak, perhaps you can spend the remainder of yard duty patrolling the bicycle area. There seems to be some confusion here."

Mrs. Boswell scanned the quiet crowd one more time, then turned on one very high heel and marched Max, Davidson and Jeremy up to the office.

The rest of recess passed quietly. It was a relief.

* * *

Mrs. Tweedie was sitting at her desk, her hands folded in front of her, when we came back in. So were Davidson, Max and Jeremy.

When we were all seated, Mrs. Tweedie spoke.

"As you know, three students have had their bicycles vandalized. The police will be conducting an investigation. You are to leave it to them. Do you hear me?" She looked around the classroom. "Max?" she asked. "Davidson?"

Max nodded. Davidson muttered something that sounded like "Okay," or maybe it was "No way." I couldn't tell from where I sat. Jeremy still didn't look up.

"Good," Mrs. Tweedie said. She took a deep breath and said, "Next Friday we'll be having our Halloween party and, of course, the costume parade for the younger children. Anyone who wants to bring a treat is welcome to do so. Now, we'll continue with our reading."

Before I even had my book on my desk, I was asked to pass a note to Davidson from Max. Moments later, a note from Julia to Jason sailed by. When Mrs. Tweedie's back was turned, Max lobbed a message to Ed. I received two notes, one from Davidson suggesting that I meet them at lunch to "make Jeremy pay" and one from Aileen telling me that I should take Jeremy to the police. There was a P.S. on the note, inviting me to a Halloween party on Friday night.

The lunch bell rang. Davidson looked around, a wolfish grin on his face.

"Jeremy, you may go to the nurse's office," Mrs. Tweedie said. He grabbed his red lunchbox and scuttled from the room. "I expect the rest of you to behave yourselves," she said. "Enjoy your lunch."

There wasn't much chance of that, I thought. Not unless Jeremy was served between two slices of bread.

* * *

One of the grade eight prefects caught me on my way into the lunchroom and asked for my advice on recapturing gerbils. By the time I'd devised a plan for him, my friends had already finished their lunches.

"Do you want to come with us?" Davidson

asked. "We're going to wait till Jeremy comes out of the nurse's office and then we're going to grab him and drag him over to the Sweeneys'. They're never there during the day."

"And then what?" I asked.

"We'll see," he said darkly.

I looked at the lunchroom monitors.

"What about them?" I asked.

"They're going to be taken care of," Davidson promised.

I opened my mouth to ask another question when one of the kids standing guard in the door-way waved at Davidson.

"He's coming!" he yelled.

Davidson nodded at the kids at the table nearest the monitors. They started jumping up and down, pounding each other on the head and shouting accusations. The monitors got sucked into an argument about who stole whose pickle and jam sandwich and which marshmallows belonged to which kid.

Davidson, Max and the other guys from my class swarmed into the hallway. I followed, my lunch forgotten.

Jeremy stood by the lunchroom door, a pack of kids pinning him to the wall.

"Wait!" he said, "Wait a minute!"

"Take him outside," Davidson howled.

Chapter 9

Justice Delayed

Jeremy swayed back and forth as hands pulled him first to one side and then to another, but always toward the far set of doors. His eyes burned black in his white face and when he saw me over the snarling heads and grappling hands, I felt his panic.

"Hunter!" he called to me. "Hunter!"

I pushed my way through the line of sightseers and yanked the first kid I could get my hands on.

"Stop," I shouted. "Wait a minute."

"Let's go, let's go," Davidson screamed. The gang propelled Jeremy down the hallway.

I ran with the pack.

"Wait!" I shouted again.

They didn't listen. The classrooms were all

empty, the staff room was around the other side of the school, and the prefect I'd talked to had gone off to follow my advice. We were on our own.

"Hunter!" Jeremy called once more.

There was another scuffle once we got to the far set of doors. I peeled a couple of kids off Jeremy's back and someone's watch scraped across my face. It made me mad. The moment we broke free of the doors, I circled the mob and went straight for Davidson, who was leading the way. I grabbed him, spun him around to face me, and clutched him just above the waist in a bear hug.

Someone laughed. A voice from the crowd yelled out, "Davidson's got a boyfriend." Davidson wasn't laughing, though, as I tightened my arms.

"Tell them to let him go," I roared. He tried to throw me off, but I'd caught him low down and he couldn't get his balance.

"Call a truce," I ordered. He huffed and panted and strained and heaved. He weighed a tonne. I knew I couldn't hold him much longer. He was kicking my legs. I brought my head up quickly and hit him under the chin. It hurt so much I wondered if I'd live. It must have hurt him too.

"Truce," he whispered.

"Louder," I shouted. No one had heard him over the cheering crowd.

"Truce!" he bellowed.

I dropped my arms and staggered back. Davidson fell to his knees, his hands cupped on his chin.

"Let go of Jeremy," I said. My head had started to ache. Max and Brent looked at Davidson. He took a deep shuddering breath and slowly got to his feet.

"Okay guys," he said. We all watched as they slowly released Jeremy. He was pale, and the collar and one sleeve of his shirt were torn. I could see scratches on his face and hands.

"I didn't do it," he said in a hoarse whisper. He cleared his throat and spoke again. "I didn't wreck those bikes."

He turned to me. "I want you to find out who did, Hunter. I'll pay you to be my detective." With trembling hands he straightened his shirt back across his shoulders and tucked it down into his jeans.

There was an excited buzz all around me. I wished my headache would disappear. I needed to do some hard thinking, but the only thing I could bring to mind was a dark, quiet room and a soft bed.

"We all know you did it," Brent shouted at Jeremy.

"No I didn't," Jeremy protested. A lump the size of a bird's egg was coming up on his forehead. "I swear I didn't."

"We have evidence," Max yelled. "One of the little kids saw you bust up my bike."

"It wasn't me," Jeremy insisted. "Hunter will prove it."

Everyone turned to stare at me.

Davidson limped over to where I stood. He came close, so close I wondered if it was going to be round two, but he stopped with the toe of his sneaker just touching the outside of my shoe. He peered into my face.

"You better get this right," he hissed. "If it isn't Diskau, then it's someone else in our class. You'd better find out who." He looked me up and down. "And you'd better find out fast."

"Just back off," I said, "and let me do my job. I don't need . . . " but I was interrupted. Ms Babiak's whistle sounded sharp and shrill.

"Boys!" she said, "Boys!" She rushed toward us, her black coat flapping behind her like the wings of a crow. "What's going on here?"

Jeremy looked at me, but didn't speak. I looked at Davidson, daring him to say anything. The rest of the crowd was silent.

"Well?" she said.

I realized that the wetness on my cheek was blood. I wiped it off with the back of my hand.

"You," she said to me. "What happened?"

The hammering inside my head made it difficult to think, but I tried. I wondered if I should tell her everything. But then I'd have Davidson and Max against me. How could I conduct an investigation if none of the witnesses would talk to me? Besides, I had things under control now.

"We were playing British Bulldog," I said.

Slowly, reluctantly, Ms Babiak said, "All right. I'll accept that for now. But I'm going to be watching you boys."

She was true to her word. Instead of continuing on her patrol, she stayed where she was, swinging the whistle in her hands, her eyes fixed on us.

Davidson glared at Jeremy and me before following Max to the side doors. Within a few minutes, Davidson was ducking and twisting, describing to his friends how he'd almost taken me down.

"We'd better meet after school," I said to Jeremy, turning and facing him for the first time.

"Okay," he said. "We can go to my house." He looked at me closely. "You do believe me, don't you?" he asked.

My head felt like a drum being pounded with a wooden mallet.

"I guess so," I said. "But I wish I had more clues."

Jason ambled over to join us, a basketball balanced on the tips of his fingers, a smile on his face. He stopped smiling when he got closer.

"Wow! What happened to you?" he asked.

"What happened to you?" I shot back. "Where were you when I needed you?"

"I was talking to Julia about Aileen's party," he said. "I told her we were going."

He blushed. I sighed. It was a difficult case to begin with. It would be almost impossible without expert assistance. Jason looked from me to Jeremy and over to Davidson and his gang.

"Did you guys have a fight or something?" he asked.

"Brilliant deduction," I said sarcastically. "And it ain't over yet."

Chapter 10

Jeremy Speaks

I told Jason that I would interrogate Jeremy after school and he could have the afternoon off. I thought he might want to have a talk with Ed. Instead, he offered to carry Aileen's bike home for her.

Davidson and his gang were waiting for Jeremy and me by the school gate. After sneering at Jeremy's old bike, Davidson turned to me.

"You've got one week," he said.

"And then what?" I asked, looking at the dark purple bruise on the tip of his chin.

"Then Max's older brother and his friends take you apart," he said.

I hadn't figured on that. Still, it was crucial not to show any fear.

"No problem," I said. "Just leave me alone and let me get on with the job."

"Hope he pays you enough," Davidson laughed. "You're going to need plastic surgery when Max's brother finishes with you."

I considered this on my way over to Jeremy's. Considered it until I hit the first pothole and my head threatened to explode. Then I concentrated on my steering instead.

* * *

Jeremy's house was empty, not only of people but of things. There was no carpet on the floor, no extra cushions on the couch or the matching chair, no curtains beside the living room blinds. At first I thought they were still moving in, but then I realized that the house was incredibly clean. The hardwood floor shone. There wasn't a dust ball anywhere.

"It's because of my asthma," Jeremy said, his eyes following mine. "I'm allergic to dust."

"Don't ever come to my place," I said. "My parents can't agree on who should do the housework so it only gets done when it's an emergency. When my grandmother's coming over or something."

"My mom vacuums every morning before she goes to work," Jeremy said. "But I have to make sure there isn't any mess anywhere because she only has twenty minutes."

"What about your father?" I asked. It's no good being a detective if you don't ask questions.

"He lives in Markham," Jeremy said. "With his second wife and their kids. Do you want a snack?"

I followed him into the small, shining kitchen. The counter was clean, the table was clean. I was willing to bet that even the top of the fridge was clean. I wondered if I could get my parents over here to meet Jeremy's mother.

"What do you want?" Jeremy asked.

"What do you have?" I asked. I hoped that a mother who liked to clean was a mother who liked to cook. Homemade cookies and cakes. Apple pie. Double chocolate fudge.

Jeremy opened the fridge.

"Mostly vegetables in here," he said, "Milk, juice, sliced ham, leftover meatloaf." He opened a cupboard door. "Ketchup, marmalade, sardines, instant soup, crackers, tea bags, pickles. Want some crackers?"

"Okay," I said.

He handed me a stack of ten crackers and sat at the table. I took the top cracker off the stack and wedged it in my mouth. It was tasteless and dry. Puffs of crumb escaped when I opened my mouth to ask for a drink of water.

"Do you have any Tylenol?" I added.

"Sure," he said. I followed him into the predictably neat bathroom. There was a huge medicine cabinet set in the wall above the toilet and it was packed with more boxes and foil packets and vials and tubes than I'd ever seen in my life.

Jeremy rummaged through one of the shelves.

"We have Aspirin and Anacin and extra-strength acetominophen and Padasol with dextramethorphane," he said. "What do you want?"

So many pain-killers, only one box of tasteless crackers. I sighed. "That's okay, Jeremy. I think I'll just wait till I get home."

Down the hallway came a steady bubbling noise.

"What's that?" I asked.

"My pets," he said. "Come see."

I followed him into his (of course) neat and tiny bedroom. The noise was coming from the aquariums that lined the walls. One was huge, about two metres by a metre and a half. There were several smaller ones, including one on his desk. Small, vividly striped fish swam in one. Some dark fish swam in another.

"This," he said, pointing at the big aquarium, "is my favourite tank. I've got a couple of sunfishes and a firemouth," he pointed out a spotted fish with a red mouth and belly. "His name is Fury because he bit my mother's finger once when she was taking out a shell to clean it. He doesn't bite me, of course. He recognizes me."

"What's that?" I interrupted, pointing at a long, shadowy shape half-submerged in sand.

"Don't touch the glass!" he said. "They can feel the vibrations. That's my spiny eel. I call him Spike. He's hunting."

It looked more like sleeping to me, but before I could ask any questions, Jeremy had gone on to another aquarium.

" . . . Darter and Drifter and Dancer. They're all neon tetras. I used to have another one called Daffy, but he died."

The bright little fish looked identical to me. I wondered how he could tell them apart.

He moved on. The bubbling of the air filters turned my headache up a notch.

"Listen," I said, "This is all really interesting and everything but we have to talk about the bikes at school."

Jeremy turned away from me and his voice faded.

"Yeah, I guess so," he said.

"Tell me what you think," I said.

"Well, it wasn't me," he said flatly.

"Our witness says he saw someone who was about your size wearing a red jacket."

He shrugged.

"Maybe it was Renner Dhali. Or Julia Chung," he suggested.

I shook my head.

"The kid who saw it may not know much, but there's no way he'd confuse you with Renner or Julia," I said.

"I don't know," he said after a moment's thought. "I don't pay attention to any of that stuff. It's not really interesting to me, if you know what I mean."

I nodded my head. That was the way I felt about things like movie stars and running shoes. But Jeremy seemed to carry his lack of curiosity too far. Surely there was more to life than neon tetras and spiny eels?

Jeremy started wheezing again.

"I'd just like my life to get back to normal," he said and coughed.

I could agree with him on that.

"What about your asthma?" I said.

"I'll be better once the weather gets colder. The frost will kill the leaf mould and I'll be okay."

I hoped it happened soon. The whistling and squeaking noises were getting on my nerves.

"Don't you think you should take some medicine?" I asked.

"I'm just going to. About the money, Hunter . . . "

I interrupted him.

"We'll talk about it later," I said.

"Thanks, Hunter," he wheezed. He held the front door open for me. "I knew you'd help."

I could hear him coughing as he closed the door behind me. I got on my bike and cycled carefully home.

Chapter 11

A Saturday Afternoon at Ed's House

Aileen called on Saturday morning. Unfortunately, Thomas answered the phone.

"Hunter," he yelled. "It's your *girlfriend.*"

I grabbed the receiver from him, jabbing my elbow at his ribs. He knew it was coming, though, and twisted out of reach. As Aileen talked about insurance money and a new bike, Thomas danced around me singing some childish rhyme about people in a tree kissing. I pulled the cord as straight as I could, trying to get the few extra centimetres that would bring him into range.

"And I just wanted to make sure you're coming to my Halloween party," Aileen continued.

"Yeah, yeah," I said, as I aimed a kick at

Thomas, who had come a little closer. "Talk to you later. Bye."

"You are coming?" she asked.

My kick just brushed him. The doorbell rang. Thomas went to answer it, still singing.

"Sure and good-bye," I said. "Gotta go."

"Bye," she said wistfully.

As I hung up the phone, Thomas followed Jason into the kitchen.

"Is Hunter there?" Thomas squeaked in a feeble imitation of Aileen's voice, his eyes rolling.

I swatted him on the back of the head as we left the house.

"Someday we've got to get that kid," Jason said.

* * *

"Let's go see Ed," Jason suggested, when I brought my bike around to the front of the house to join him.

"Good idea," I replied.

It was another hot, sunny afternoon. Everywhere people were raking and bagging coloured leaves. But Ed's house looked deserted. Neither of his parents' cars was in the driveway. We stood on the front steps and listened to the doorbell chimes echo inside. Several fliers were stuck through the front railing.

"I guess they've gone somewhere," I said.

We were halfway down the steps when the front door opened. Ed stood in the doorway, wearing a

T-shirt and underpants, his hair rumpled.

He rubbed his eyes and yawned. "I was asleep," he said. "What do you want?"

"It's 1:57," I said, looking at my watch.

"Oh," he mumbled.

"Can we come in?" Jason asked.

"I guess so," Ed said. He stepped back into the hall to let us through the door.

The front hall was littered with boots and shoes. We followed Ed into the kitchen. There was an impressive stack of pizza boxes and Chinese food cartons on the counter.

Ed yawned and opened the fridge. All that was inside was a jar of pickles. He closed the fridge door and sat on a kitchen chair.

I picked a shirt off the chair closest to me and sat down. Jason leaned by a stack of pizza boxes.

"So what's up?" Ed asked, yawning again.

"I thought we could do some detective work on the bicycle thing," I said. "Make a plan."

Ed groaned. "That's all you talk about. Why don't we do something else?"

"Like what?" I asked sternly.

Ed looked at the ceiling and shrugged. "I don't know," he said.

"Maybe we could call on someone," Jason suggested.

I frowned at him. Was he deserting me too?

"Who?" Ed said, scratching his head. A cloud of

dandruff flakes hung in the air, then settled on his shoulders. Tomato sauce speckled the front of his T-shirt.

"We could see what Renner's up to," Jason suggested. He picked at the cold mozzarella stuck to the top of the nearest pizza box.

Now I knew what Jason was doing. I watched Ed closely to see how he would react. He continued scratching his head.

"I'm hungry," he said after a moment's thought.

That didn't sound like true love to me.

"What's with the mess?" I asked, pointing to the boxes and dirty plates.

Ed looked at them as if seeing them for the first time. "I'd better load the dishwasher," he said. He got to his feet and opened the door of the dishwasher. An overpowering stink billowed out.

"Oh gross," Jason groaned. He pinched his nose shut. I could see furry mould on the plates nearest the door of the dishwasher.

"We forgot to run it," Ed said. He dumped in several handfuls of soap and started the machine running. Jason was still waving the air in front of his face.

"Are your parents away?" I asked. I remembered the time three years ago when they had gone on vacation and left Ed and his older brother, Simon, by themselves. Ed's socks were so disgusting by the time they got back that his mother threw them out and made him spend his baseball card money buying new ones.

"My dad's out shopping," Ed said. "I hope he gets back soon. I'm starving."

"What do you want to do in the meantime?" I asked. Ed's obsession with food was boring. Jason chewed on the chunk of cold mozzarella he had pried loose.

"I don't know," Ed said. "Maybe I'll have a nap."

"Then we'll be going," I said as I got to my feet. Ed followed Jason and me to the front door.

"Maybe we'll see you tomorrow," I said from the front steps.

"Maybe," he said and yawned. He didn't sound like he cared much one way or the other.

We grabbed our bikes from the front lawn and cruised down the street.

"He doesn't look like a man in love to me," I said to Jason.

"I guess not," Jason said. He thought for a minute. "Maybe he's got sleeping sickness," he said.

I shook my head.

"It's something else," I said. "And when this bike business is over, I'm going to give it some serious thought."

At least, that was my plan.

Chapter 12

Another Opportunity

Davidson strutted into the classroom on Monday morning several minutes late.

"My dad drove me and my new bike to school," he announced, as he handed his late slip to Mrs. Tweedie. "He's going to talk to the principal about security."

"That's nice," Mrs. Tweedie said. "Math books out please. Let's take another look at those problems on page forty-one."

We pulled our math books out. In the middle of the third problem, a ball of paper hit my elbow.

"Hunter," I read, "My dad paid $389.49 plus tax for my new bike. If anything happens to it, he's going to hold you personally responsible." It was signed "Davidson J. Pruitt." At the bottom it said:

"P.S. We told Max's brother all about you."

I could feel Davidson staring at me, but I wasn't going to let him know that I was worried. I smiled instead and nodded. He turned away.

I caught Jeremy looking at me, a troubled expression on his round face. I nodded to him, too, and then to Jason and Max, who had also turned to stare. I felt like my head was on a spring.

Mrs. Tweedie announced a snap math quiz. A wave of groans rolled through the classroom, but she pretended not to hear. In the middle of the sixth question, she sat down abruptly.

"I think we'll resume work on our three-dimensional shapes instead," she announced. "Remember please which ratio you are using."

I couldn't see why she'd suddenly changed her mind about the quiz. Had she remembered that the dry cleaning needed to be picked up?

I went over to the window ledge to get our pyramid. The straws in the equilateral triangle on one corner of the base had slipped loose. I picked it up gently and carried it over to my desk. Jason helped Julia bring the box of straws.

"I'm going to get a lime-green bike this time," Aileen said as she grabbed a ball of string.

"I hope Jeremy doesn't wreck mine," Julia said. "My father says he can't afford to buy me a new one, not even with the insurance."

"We still don't know it was Jeremy," I said.

Aileen looked at me and frowned.

"Hunter," she said, "we all know it's Jeremy. The whole school knows. And just because he's paying you doesn't mean he's not guilty."

Before I could correct her, there was a shout and a sudden crash of splintering glass from the other end of the room. I turned to see Ed standing by the art supply centre, holding a lid in his hand, surrounded by a puddle of glass and white glue. His sweatpants were dappled from the knees to the ankles. His sneakers were soaked.

"Someone forgot to screw the lid on the jar," he said.

Mrs. Tweedie heaved a huge sigh.

"Go to the washroom and wash the glue off," she said. Ed trudged out of the room, his sneakers squelching. "Aileen," she continued, "would you please go to the custodians' office and tell them we need their help." Aileen ran out of the classroom, taking care not to step in any of Ed's puddles.

"I got glue splashed all down my leg," Renner complained.

"Go to the washroom and wash it off then," Mrs. Tweedie snapped. "Brent, get away from there," she called. Brent had been edging forward and was standing on the edge of the field of glass and glue.

"I just want to see if the tops are on the other jars," he offered.

"Leave it alone," Mrs. Tweedie said.

"I could squeeze past Davidson's tower thing and reach the box," he said again. As he spoke, he stuck one foot forward and angled his body around past the poorly built, leaning tower that Davidson and his group had been working on.

"Get back!" Mrs. Tweedie spoke sharply. Too sharply. Brent lost his balance, caught the tower with his elbow and knocked it over into the shards and glue.

"How dare you!" Davidson roared.

"You broke it," Max shouted.

Brent stepped back into the circle of witnesses.

"I didn't mean to," he said, a wide grin on his face. He looked down at his feet. His shoelaces were untied, and one lace was heavy and wet with glue.

Mrs. Tweedie's face was red and her voice was squeaky.

"You had better take your shoes off. You can spend the rest of the day in your sock feet."

"Okay." Brent pried one sticky shoe off.

"His feet stink!" Renner shrieked.

"Take them off in the hallway," Mrs. Tweedie said.

Brent limped to the door, holding one stained sneaker by the dripping lace. Aileen reappeared with Fred, who pushed a mop in a bucket on wheels.

"Thank you, Mr. Bayley," Mrs. Tweedie said.

"As you can see, there's been an accident." She pointed to the corner of the room. "You may all go back to work," she said to the class.

Jason and I moved desks out of the way so Fred could wheel the bucket closer to the spill. Davidson and Max rushed to help Fred rescue their shattered tower from the puddle on the floor, while Julia explained to Aileen exactly what had happened. Ed wandered back into the room. His trousers were wet to the knee and his socks had holes in them.

"The top was loose," he said.

Jeremy coughed. Davidson carried the wreckage of the tissue paper tower over to the garbage can and dumped it in. Jeremy coughed again. And again.

Mrs. Tweedie turned from her examination of Fred's work to look at Jeremy.

"You'd better go up to the nurse's office," she said.

Davidson and Max stopped moaning about their ruined project and stared at Jeremy. So did Julia and Aileen. And Jason. And everyone else. I'm sure we were all thinking about the same thing: Davidson's new bike.

Fred's mop continued to sweep back and forth across the floor in ever-widening circles.

"I'm okay," Jeremy mumbled. "I'll go at recess."

"Don't be silly," Mrs. Tweedie said. "Now's a

good time. You don't look very well."

She was right. He looked grey. Whether this was from asthma or fear, I couldn't tell.

"I'll go with him," I offered.

"Why?" Mrs. Tweedie said. "He's perfectly capable of going on his own."

"I can make sure he gets there safely and I'll stay with him until he's ready to come back," I said.

"Of course he'll get there safely," she said. She frowned at Jeremy, who was bent over his desk, his shoulders twitching as he tried to muffle the coughs with his hands. Fred stood his mop in the bucket and wheeled it round the desks and out the door.

"Thank you, Mr. Bayley," Mrs. Tweedie called after him. Then she turned back to the class. "I think it's time we all got back to work," she said. "Off you go, Jeremy."

Jeremy stumbled after Fred. Mrs. Tweedie rambled on about ratios and fractions. I kept my eyes on the clock behind her. I was waiting for recess. And I wasn't the only one.

Chapter 13

Another Disaster

We stampeded for the doors when the bell finally rang. Mrs. Tweedie caught Davidson and his group as they charged past her.

"We must discuss what to do about your math project," I heard her say.

I couldn't wait to get to the playground. But when I got there, I wished I go could right back inside again. Or go on a two-week vacation, starting immediately. For Davidson's flashy new bike was smashed. It was ripped. It was slashed, scraped and wrenched. And the bike next to it, a little blue one with streamers attached to the handle grips, had been slashed too, as if in passing.

I groaned, but no one heard me. The sound was lost in the howls of rage that surrounded me. The kid who owned the blue bike trotted up to see what was happening and then burst into tears. His older sister and her friends put their arms around him and led him away.

"What are you going to do, Hunter?" Jason asked.

I shrugged my shoulders, at a sudden loss for words.

"Davidson's going to kill you," Jason said.

"Actually, he's going to make me pay for the bike first and then he's going to kill me," I said grimly.

"Maybe he won't kill you," Jason said hopefully. "You beat him the last time."

"I don't think it will be one-on-one," I said. "I expect I'll get mugged. I . . . "

I didn't finish the sentence. I couldn't. Davidson was pushing his way toward the battered bike, Max following a few steps behind. The crowd melted out of his way. In a moment they'd pulled back, leaving Davidson and Max facing the tortured bike. I held my breath.

"Wow!" Davidson whistled. "That Diskau guy is really twisted."

Max peered at Davidson anxiously.

"Look what he did to that bike," Davidson continued.

"It's not yours?" Max asked in a squeak.

"Naw," Davidson answered. "It saw it at The

Sports Stop Shop for $229.99, but I didn't like the fluorescent yellow stripes. Looks like Disgusting Diskau didn't either."

One of the grade eight teachers, Mr. Feeney, a big barrel of a man dressed in a chalk-stained black suit and maroon knitted vest, lumbered around the corner of the building. It didn't surprise me that Mrs. Boswell had put him on yard duty. His size alone made people think twice about causing trouble. He blew his whistle and waved his arms around. The little kids scattered.

"Mullet and Chomsky," he said, pointing at a couple of kids from his class, "go up to the office and tell Mrs. Boswell that another two bikes have been vandalized. The people who own these bikes can stay. The rest of you clear off." He scowled at the crowd.

Davidson proudly led a group of kids to the far end of the playground to admire his new bike. Jason and I drew back to the corner of the building and waited to see what would happen. "Whose bike is it?" Jason asked.

I shook my head.

"Beats me," I said.

The doors flew open and a crowd stormed out, led by Mrs. Boswell. Her black patent leather high heels clicked crisply on the pavement. The vice-principal trotted after her. So did two of the office secretaries, Fred Bayley and the school nurse.

Jeremy was the last person out the door.

"My bike," he screamed. He ran over to it and tried to stand it up. "My bike. My new bike. It's my new bike."

The back wheel rim had been smashed in, so the bike no longer balanced. It tilted crazily toward Jeremy, held upright only by the chain that attached it to the fence.

"Where is he?" Jeremy cried. He dropped the bike and turned on the crowd. A couple of kids giggled. The rest stood silent. "Where's Davidson Pruitt? I'm going to kill him!"

"Stop that," Mrs. Boswell snapped. "Stop that right now. I will call the police and inform them that I expect this matter to be dealt with promptly."

She glared at Jeremy and at the crowd, then marched back inside. If I was a policeman faced with Mrs. Boswell, I'd do my job promptly too.

Mr. Feeney blew his whistle a few more times and people slowly drifted away.

I strode over and grabbed Jeremy by the arm. He was muttering about Davidson and his bike.

"Cool it," I said.

"It was a birthday present from my father." He turned to me. "I never see him. I never talk to him. This was his first visit since August." Jeremy was almost shouting now. "He came down on Saturday afternoon and took me out and bought me this bike. And look at it now. What do I do? Tell me? What do I do?"

"You don't go looking for Davidson," I said.

"Here he comes," Jason warned.

Davidson strolled toward us, his hands tucked in the back pockets of his jeans. The gang that was with him pressed closer to hear what he was going to say.

"Don't think it's going to work," he said in a smooth voice. "Trashing your own bike isn't going to get you off the hook."

Jeremy pushed up against him. "What do you mean?" he cried.

Mr. Feeney approached, whistle poised.

"I mean, Dis-gust Face, that I know you did it. And I'm going to see that you . . . "

I couldn't listen to him any longer.

"You've got to be crazy," I said. "Do you seriously think that Jeremy totally obliterated his own bike just to make himself look innocent?"

Mr. Feeney was upon us. He waved his arms like a windmill and blew the whistle repeatedly. It was almost impossible to hear anything above the piercing squeal.

"So he's crazy," Davidson screamed.

I shook my head in despair and drew Jeremy and Jason away with me. When we got around the far side of the climbing equipment I said, "Look at the bright side. At least you've proved your innocence. No one but Davidson could come up with a dumb idea like that."

I was wrong.

* * *

As we filed back into the building, I overheard Max whispering that Jeremy had destroyed his bike to collect the insurance money. In the classroom, I listened to Renner explain to Ed that crazy people can't tell one thing from another so Jeremy probably didn't even know it was his own bike when he attacked it.

I scattered a fistful of notes telling people that only a complete idiot would destroy his own bike, and asking if people really thought Jeremy was a complete idiot. I got a surprising number of notes back saying yes, and a dangerous maniac, too.

At 2:45 that afternoon, the police arrived. I was interested to see what crime detection and interviewing techniques they'd use. First they talked to Davidson, Max, Aileen and Jeremy. Then they called an assembly in the gym. Mrs. Boswell spoke first, at great length, about co-operation. Next to speak was Constable Barnsduer. He talked briefly about co-operation. And that was it.

I was shocked. I knew the police were busy with dangerous criminals twenty-four hours a day, but I thought our case deserved more attention. From the fiery look in Mrs. Boswell's eyes, she thought so too. I wondered if she was going to give Constable Barnsduer a detention.

That was when I realized that it all depended on me.

Chapter 14

A Brilliant Plan

For the third morning in a row, Jason and I stood guard by the chained bicycles. Jeremy stood with us, lost in thought. His neon tetras looked pale, he told us, and Dancer had a yellow spot on the base of her tail.

Davidson and his gang lounged by the side doors of the school. Max Goldhar was throwing his fluorescent yellow tennis ball into the air and bumping people out of the way as he lunged to catch it. Brent Wexler was hanging on the edge of the group. Max tossed the ball high and took three quick steps to get under it, pushing Brent off his feet. Brent, his smiling face turned toward us, knocked Max off balance on his next toss. Everyone scrambled for the loose ball.

It was a typical scene, except for two things. Ed wasn't there. And Jason and I were in exile.

"I've had enough," I said. "We're never going to solve the case this way. Our time's running out."

"It happened really quickly," Jeremy agreed. "One day Daffy had two spots on his tail fin, the next day he was dead."

"Not your fish," I said. "This bicycle stuff. I'm tired of watching the bikes all the time. There are plenty of other things I could be doing." Jason nodded agreement, his eyes on the far side of the building where Aileen and Julia stood.

"We've got to make the bicycle slasher show himself. We can't just wait for him to make a mistake," I continued.

"Maybe I should have taken him out of the aquarium right away," Jeremy said. "Maybe Dancer wouldn't have caught whatever it is."

"I think we should try a stake-out," I said. The moment I spoke, I realized it was a brilliant idea. "Let's put someone's bike out where we can watch it and catch this guy in the act."

I looked at the other two. Jeremy was frowning, probably still brooding about his fish. Jason's face was twisted. Before I could ask what the problem was, he sneezed.

I looked at the spit on the sleeve of my sweatshirt.

"Watch it!" I said.

He nodded, threw his head back and sneezed twice.

"I think I've got a cold," he said.

"Well, I don't want it," I said. "Keep it to yourself. Now listen, about the bike. When do you think your dad will get you another?" I asked Jeremy.

"I don't know," Jeremy said. "I heard my mother yelling at him on the phone."

I waited for him to continue. When he didn't speak, I decided to give him a nudge.

"So, what did she say?"

Red patches covered his cheeks.

"A lot of stuff," he said. He was quiet again and then said, "I don't think I'm going to get a new bike for a while."

"What about you?" I turned to Jason.

In place of a Kleenex, he rubbed the sleeve of his jean jacket under his nose.

"What about me?" he asked.

"Maybe we should use your bike as the bait," I said.

"I think we should use yours," he said, sniffing. "Your bike looks better than mine. It will tempt him more."

My bike *was* in better condition. Jason never bothered using the kickstand, so his wheel rims and pedals were scratched from hitting the ground every time he dumped it.

But I still wasn't sure using my bike was a good idea.

"Everyone knows which bike is mine," I said. "The bicycle slasher won't attack a bike that belongs to me."

Jason sneezed.

"Why not?" he said.

I looked at him in surprise.

"Why not?" I echoed.

"Yeah, why not?" he repeated.

"Because he won't want to make me angry," I said. "Or he'd know I'd get him for sure."

"I thought you already said you were going to get him," Jason said. He sniffed twice.

"That doesn't mean I want to sacrifice my bike," I said.

Jason sniffed again.

"Don't you have a Kleenex?" I asked.

"Nope," he said.

"Or maybe I should have changed the water. Maybe it's polluted with something," Jeremy mused.

"Okay," I said to Jason. "We'll use my bike. But the plan had better be foolproof."

"You can do it," he said to me.

The morning bell rang. I wondered if I was coming down with Jason's cold. Even in the hot sun, I didn't feel so good any more.

* * *

During novel study, I worked out my plan. At recess I'd announce that I was going to park my bike at a different section of the fence because I thought it would be safer there. That would make the bicycle slasher think that I was afraid of him. I chose a location near the play equipment shed. That would give me a good place to hide.

I decided to try the plan the next day. I figured Jason and I could slip out in the confusion of the class Halloween party and be in place long before the slasher arrived.

Ordinarily, I'd have asked Ed to keep an eye on Jeremy. It was crucial to have a witness to prove that Jeremy was somewhere else when the bicycle slasher struck. That way, even if by some incredible chance the bicycle slasher escaped Jason and me, people wouldn't think Jeremy was guilty.

But Ed didn't seem interested in detective work anymore and I couldn't trust him to do the job properly. So I talked to Aileen instead. She and Julia were delighted to help.

All that remained was to tempt the bicycle slasher. Before I approached Davidson's gang, I checked to see where the teacher on yard duty was. I had no intention of getting into a fight that was six or seven against one. As it turned out, I needn't have worried. Mr. Feeney had posted himself just metres away from the gang. He rocked slowly back and forth, his arms folded over his belly, his eyes unblinking.

"The great detective's come to join us," Davidson jeered when he saw me.

"Where's your police escort?" Max asked.

"I guess I'm lucky my bike's an old wreck and my parents are too cheap to buy me a new one," Brent said. "Otherwise, I'd have to depend on Hunter to save me!"

I sighed.

"Look, you guys," I said, "I don't like this any more than you do . . . "

"Making big money, are you?" Davidson interrupted.

"And I'm going to move my bike to a safer place so it won't get damaged," I continued.

"I don't think this guy is interested in crummy bikes like yours," Brent said coldly.

"It's not crummy," I replied. "For one thing, it has great brakes."

"Big deal," Davidson said. "Mine has better ones."

"Anyway," I insisted, trying not to let my anger show, "I just thought I'd let you know that I'm going to park it by the kindergarten entrance."

"Your bike only has twelve gears," Davidson continued. "It's pathetic. Who'd want it?"

"What's so safe about the kindergarten entrance?" Brent asked.

"Yeah," Max sneered. He threw his tennis ball at my feet so that it bounced up under my nose. "What's so safe about the kindergarten entrance?"

I stepped away from the ball and thought quickly.

"The kindergarten teacher's going to keep an eye out," I said. "She promised the parents of the little kids that she'd watch to make sure their bikes weren't touched."

"Hunter's going to park his bike by the baby bikes," Davidson crooned. "Isn't that cute!"

"Maybe one of the kindergarten kiddies can find your bicycle slasher for you," Brent suggested.

"It may not work," I said. I didn't want the slasher to be scared away by the thought of Mrs. Masham spying on the bikes. "She's awfully busy with all those little kids. And she sometimes leaves the room. During the costume parade, for example," I said, with a sudden stroke of genius. "Pass the word along, will you, that it's a safer place to stash your bike most of the time. Although I guess it'll be unsupervised while the costume parade's going on."

I'd done it. That was sure to tempt the slasher out into the open. Where Jason and I would be waiting.

I was still smiling when the bell rang.

Chapter 15

The Trap is Set

The next day I put my plan into action. Thomas and I went home at lunch to get our Halloween stuff. My mother spent the whole hour pinning Thomas into his dinosaur costume. He squirmed and twitched and moaned that he was too hot and that he wanted blood around his dinosaur mouth to make him look scary.

I needed to be able to see clearly and move quickly, so I slung my binoculars around my neck, stuffed a book about birds in my pocket, put on a silly hat of my father's and rode my bike back to school.

I whizzed past princesses, skeletons and large furry animals. The wind had picked up, plucking at black capes and bright spangled skirts. A Minnie Mouse at the corner of Broadway and Southlea had her ears blown off. A slice of pizza ran down the street chasing the pepperoni rounds that skipped ahead of it. I met Aileen and Julia at the side of the music portable, as we had agreed. They had sprayed iridescent green and purple streaks in their hair and put on gobs of makeup.

I tried not to stare as I gave them their final instructions.

" . . . and if he goes in the boys' washroom," I said, "wait outside the door for him."

Aileen wrinkled up her face.

"How disgusting," she said. Her fluorescent green skeleton earrings danced up and down.

"I didn't say you had to go in, did I?" I said. "Look, it's really important that you stay with him. That's the only way you can give him an alibi."

"Just so long as I don't have to talk to him," Aileen said. "He wrecked my bike, after all."

I was about to explain that we were out to prove his innocence, when she suddenly winced and put a hand to her eye. "Ouch," she said. She detached a furry black spider from her eyelashes. But it had about thirty legs, not just eight.

"My eyelashes keep coming off," she explained. "Come on Julia, let's get some more glue."

I watched them run into the school and hoped they'd been paying attention.

Davidson and his gang were the next to arrive.

Davidson was wearing a latex monster mask and a bushy white wig. I thought of congratulating him on the improvement but decided against it. Max was dressed like a mummy, trailing wisps of white sheet. Brent was another monster type. He had a set of fangs that he kept spitting out and pushing back in again.

I'd arranged to meet Jason by the same portable. I almost didn't recognize him. He'd sprinkled white powder in his hair and combed it straight up. White paste covered his whole face, except for his lips, which he'd coloured black. Around his neck was a heavy noose. He held the end of the rope in his hand.

"You look great," I said.

"Thanks," he grinned. The inside of his mouth glistened like an open wound against the white and black makeup.

"I've talked to Aileen and Julia and they know what to do," I said.

"Great," he said and grinned again. I felt my stomach turn. I hoped he wasn't going to spend all afternoon smiling.

The bell rang.

* * *

Ed was called to the office while Mrs. Tweedie was taking attendance. I could hear excited whispers around me as he slowly got to his feet and picked up his hockey stick.

"You can leave that here," Mrs. Tweedie said.

He balanced the stick against the goalie mask on his desk and trudged out of the room.

"I heard that Simon's in trouble again," Renner whispered to Aileen.

"Silence, please," Mrs. Tweedie said. She listed off the remaining names in a shrill voice, then asked Jason to bring the sheet up to the office. I nodded at Jason on his way out. He nodded back. I'd meet him by the shed in a few minutes.

"I have a few announcements to make," Mrs. Tweedie said. Her hands plucked at the waistband of her skirt while she talked. "The police have told Mrs. Boswell that they will be back to conduct their investigation at some time in the future. They didn't say when. That means we still have a problem on our hands . . . "

"Hunter's going to handle it," Davidson said loudly. He slouched in his chair.

"And my brother's going to help," Max said. He slouched in imitation of Davidson.

"Excuse me," Mrs. Tweedie said and scowled at them. "I believe I was talking first. I expect you all to behave yourselves while the police are compiling evidence."

"They won't do a thing," Brent sneered.

"I am talking," Mrs. Tweedie shrieked.

I could see Aileen shaking her head, the skeletons dancing from side to side.

"I heard Mrs. Tweedie's husband left home," I heard Renner whisper to Julia.

"I'm not surprised," Julia whispered back.

"On another matter . . . " Mrs. Tweedie continued. We never learned what the other matter was. The intercom crackled and the vice-principal announced the beginning of the costume parade.

"Party time!" Davidson shouted.

Everyone jumped up and ran to get bags of candy and popcorn. I stopped by Jeremy's desk on my way to the door. He wasn't wearing a costume, but stood pale and silent by the side of his desk while people chattered around him.

"You stay with Aileen and Julia," I said. "Don't let them out of your sight."

"Dancer died," he said. "When I woke up this morning, she was floating on the surface. And Drifter has two spots on his tail."

"That's too bad," I said. "You remember to stick with Aileen and Julia. It's important."

I did a quick head count from the doorway to make sure that everyone was there and then slipped out into the hall. In the distance I could hear the chirping voices of the kindergarten class as they started the parade. I sidled down the hallway as quietly as any ghost, slipped through the double doors and fled around the side of the school to meet up with Jason by the shed.

"What took you so long?" he said, as I slid into place beside him.

"I came as soon as I could," I said.

He sneezed and rubbed his nose against the sleeve of his black shirt. A small pink moustache appeared where he wiped the white makeup away.

"Quiet," I whispered.

"I can't help it," he hissed.

"When you feel a sneeze coming on, pinch the bottom of your nose," I whispered.

"It doesn't work. I still sneeze," he hissed, slightly louder this time.

"Pinch it *hard*," I advised.

"My nose is sore from all the blowing I've been doing," he said. "It hurts when I pinch it."

"Ssshh!" I said. "He'll hear you."

"What are you going to wear to Aileen's party?" Jason asked and sneezed again.

I glared at him.

"All right, I'll pinch it next time," he said.

I paused to listen to the silence. I could hear the traffic on Eglinton, two blocks away. I peeked around the shed. Still no one coming.

"My regular stuff," I said. "Nothing unusual."

"Me too," Jason said quickly. "Just ordinary stuff."

Suddenly I heard what I'd been waiting for. The squeak of the double doors as they were pushed open. Someone was coming. I peered around the side of the shed, my binoculars ready.

"Who is it?" Jason breathed in my ear.

I slumped against the side of the shed and sank down onto my heels. The worst had happened. I had discovered the identity of the slasher. My good friend Ed was coming across the playground. *Ed.*

Chapter 16

A New Suspect

Jason stepped over me and looked around the side of the shed.

"Hunter," he said in alarm. "It's Ed!"

"I know," I said, my face in my hands. It was all clear to me now. Ed's strange behaviour, his lack of interest in the bicycle slasher, his refusal to reenact the crime before Jonathan, our witness. He didn't have a red jacket, true, but he had a red sweatshirt, wore it all the time. I thought back to the morning when Davidson's bike was smashed. Was Ed wearing the red sweatshirt? I could see him in my mind's eye, hunched in his chair, as Mrs. Tweedie called on him to do the math problem. Yes, he was.

"He's looking around," Jason said, confusion in

his voice, as he leaned farther away from the side of the shed.

"He's waving, he's coming toward us," he said. "Hunter? Could it really be Ed?"

I nodded sadly. All the pieces fit together. I remembered the time Jeremy's bike was busted. Had Ed deliberately loosened the cap on the bottle of glue to give himself an excuse to leave the classroom?

Ed lumbered around the side of the shed, tripping over my feet, almost landing in my lap.

"What are you doing?" he asked.

"What are *you* doing?" I shouted, my voice hot.

"Me?" he said. "I came out to look for you. You weren't in class and I heard what you said about your bike yesterday, so I thought maybe you were up to something and . . . "

"Maybe *I* was up to something," I interrupted him, my voice heavy with sarcasm. "Maybe *I* was up to something. What about you? How did you get yourself into this mess?"

"What mess?" he said looking around.

"Smashing up bicycles!" I said. "Destroying them! Whatever made you think you could go around bashing people's bikes!"

"Hey!" he said, but I ignored him. I was wild with rage.

"You've been my friend for years and years and years," I said. "We've been detectives together. And now you go and do something stupid like this. Crazy. I don't understand you."

"Well, I . . . " he began. I raised my voice and drowned him out.

"You'll go to court, you know. You're a criminal! Crazy!" I was waving my arms around, yelling. Jason watched, his mouth hanging open, forgetting even to sneeze.

"But I didn't do it," Ed said.

"What?" I yelled. "Don't add lying to the list! You're in real trouble, Ed. You don't need to go looking for more!"

"Really," he said. "I didn't smash the bikes."

"I believe him," Jason said to me. "I never did think it was Ed."

"Well if it wasn't you," I stared at him, my eyes stinging, "who was it?"

In the little silence that followed my question, we heard the side doors of the school squeak a second time. I put my finger to my mouth and motioned Jason and Ed to be silent. They both nodded. I peered around the side of the shed.

Another figure slid through the school doors, this one wearing a goalie mask and a huge hockey sweater. It crouched low by the side of the school. The white mask looked eerie as it flicked from side to side.

"That's my mask," Ed breathed in my ear.

I nodded.

"Who is it?" he asked.

I focused my binoculars on the figure and shrugged. There was no way of telling. I felt a roaring in my ears as the figure glided along the side of the school and paused at the edge of the building. Again the white mask looked left, then right. Suddenly it raised its right arm and I saw in its hand a flash of steel.

My breath caught in my throat. Beside me, I felt Jason tense. I put a hand out to stop him. We'd have to let the slasher get closer before we grabbed him.

The masked figure stared in our direction. I could feel its eyes shining through the slits of the mask. They fastened on the shed and I thought for a moment it had somehow figured out we were there. I wondered if it would use that knife on us and wished I had something more powerful to protect myself with than a pair of binoculars. Finally it looked away, over to where my bike was waiting, and I knew the moment was near.

From the safety of the building, the figure darted forward, right arm raised, knife gleaming.

And Jason sneezed.

The figure froze for one second, the cold blade clenched in its hand, poised to rip and tear. In the sudden silence I heard, coming from behind that white mask, the shallow wheezing that marks an asthma attack.

So it was Jeremy after all. After all my investigations, my days of guard duty, even the fighting, Davidson and his gang were right.

First Ed and then Jason sprang out from behind the shed and lunged after him. Jeremy spun on his heel and fled back to the safety of the school. He was running so fast that he crashed into the closed doors shoulder first. He stood stock still, frozen in pain, for a long second. But as Ed approached, he wrenched the door open with his left hand and slipped through.

Ed followed.

"Come on, Hunter," Jason called, holding the door open for me.

I took a slow step away from my hiding place, so filled with anger at Jeremy and myself that I could hardly see. Then I shook my head. This was no way to catch a creep. I had a job to finish and finish it I would. Jeremy Diskau would be sorry that he'd used me. I strode across the pavement and joined Jason.

Together, we entered the school and raced down the empty hallway, alert for some sign of Ed and Jeremy. In the distance we could hear the high-pitched babble of the little kids on their costume parade. It sounded like they were coming closer.

A face in a white hockey mask peered around the corner of Mr. Feeney's classroom door.

"Gotcha!" Jason shouted, as he grabbed the figure.

"Let go," a strange voice yelled. The goalie and Jason struggled in the open doorway.

"Stop!" I said. The guy was wearing the wrong hockey sweater. Jason had made a mistake.

"What is this nonsense?" Mr. Feeney shouted.

"That kid attacked me," said the voice behind the mask.

"Sorry," I said, as I pulled Jason away.

"Hunter, what are you doing?" Jason yelled. "Aren't we going to catch him?"

"Wrong goalie," I said.

"I'm going to speak to Mrs. Boswell about this," Mr. Feeney snapped as he snatched his student out of the corridor and dumped him back in the class.

"He shouldn't have been hanging around in the doorway," Jason muttered. "How was I supposed to know it wasn't him?"

"Jeremy?" I said.

Jason stopped short and grabbed my arm.

"What!" he said.

"You didn't hear him wheezing?" I asked.

"Wow!" Jason said. He narrowed his eyes. "So all this time, it was him?"

"Yeah," I said. I took a deep breath and let it out slowly. "All the time it was him."

"What are we going to do?" Jason asked.

"I don't know," I said, different varieties of

torture going through my head. "I have to think."

We were back at our own classroom by this time. Aileen and Julia ran to meet us.

"He's gone," Aileen said.

"Disappeared," Julia said.

"We just went to the washroom to glue our eyelashes on again and when we came out . . . " Aileen said.

" . . . he'd disappeared," Julia finished for her. "That was at 1:47. We checked our watches." She smiled proudly.

Jason smiled back.

I'd probably start smiling in another year or so when I'd gotten over the humiliation.

"It doesn't matter," I said, grinding my teeth. "It turns out it really was him after all." I tried to laugh it off, but the noise that came out of my mouth didn't sound like a laugh. It sounded more like gears grinding. Maybe in another two years, I'd try laughing again. First, I had some business to take care of.

"Have you seen Ed?" I asked as I scanned the room.

"No, he's not back yet," Aileen said. "And Mrs. Tweedie's starting to wonder where so many people have disappeared to."

I looked across the room at Mrs. Tweedie. She was dressed in a witch costume. As I watched, Renner gave her an orange cupcake from the tray she was passing around. Mrs. Tweedie held it in the palm of her hand and stared at it with a look of nausea on her face. Did she think there was a spider baked inside? She looked tired and she had dark rings under her eyes. But maybe she was just good at stage makeup.

"We'd better go before she sees us," I said.

"Yeah," Jason agreed.

Suddenly, the hallway was filled with tiny witches, pink ballerinas and drooling monsters. The costume parade had arrived.

I backed out of the way of a mouse with a broken tail. A magician in a top hat that came down over his eyes stepped on my foot.

I pushed my way through the crowd, Jason at my heels.

"Hi, Hunter," a pirate said. He hit me on the arm with his plastic sword.

"Watch it, Derek," I said. "You be careful."

Mrs. Tweedie called my name. I pretended I couldn't hear her and dodged around a cardboard-box robot and a devil in red underwear who was dragging a plastic pitchfork behind him.

A fuzzy green lump with wobbly scales and a lop-sided head barred my path.

"You're going the wrong way," Thomas said, his eyes squinting through the dinosaur's mouth.

"Don't be stupid," I said and I stepped around him.

"Hunter! Jason!" I heard Mrs. Tweedie call again.

Thomas grabbed hold of me with one felt claw and hung on.

"Your teacher's calling you," he said.

"Let go," I hissed.

Jason grabbed Thomas's claw and yanked it away.

"They're hurting me. They're hurting me," Thomas screamed.

He jerked his stubby arm free of Jason's grip, but lost his balance and fell backward into the arms of an angel. His arm knocked her halo the length of the hall like a golden frisbee. The angel collapsed under his weight, her wings bent, the coathangers poking through the white cloth like broken bones.

Mrs. Bertram, the grade one teacher, bustled forward and swept the weeping angel into a big, warm hug.

"Don't worry, Christie," she said. "We'll fix it." The class formed a shocked circle around Jason and me and their two crying classmates.

Mrs. Tweedie appeared. Davidson and Max and the rest of the class crowded behind her.

"Way to go, Hunter," Davidson called.

I couldn't hear the other insults he shouted because Thomas was wailing so loudly he sounded like an ambulance siren. He knew what Jason and

I would do to him when we got home. I almost couldn't hear Mrs. Bertram and Mrs. Tweedie letting us know what they thought of our behaviour.

"Hunter! Jason! I'm shocked at this display . . . "

"Hunter! I'm surprised that you and your friend . . . "

They had to shout above Thomas' screeching and that brought Mr. Feeney and his class out to investigate the noise.

"Not those two boys!" he roared when he saw us. "I've spoken to them already this afternoon! Assaulting students. What kind of behaviour is this?"

I thought it couldn't get much worse. But it did.

" . . . send you straight downstairs to Mrs. Boswell's office!"

" . . . see what Mrs. Boswell has to say to this!"

" . . . and if those two hooligans were in my class, I'd take them to see Mrs. Boswell myself."

Ten minutes later, Jason and I found ourselves sitting on two straight-back chairs in the office, waiting for Mrs. Boswell. That's where we spent afternoon recess and the remaining hour of class time. Still sitting in those chairs, supposedly thinking about the stinging remarks Mrs. Boswell had made and her threat of unpleasant consequences if we misbehaved again.

I don't know what Jason thought about during

those long uncomfortable minutes, but I reviewed my career as a detective. I decided it was time for a change. I'd become a scientist. No one ever got into trouble quietly mixing chemicals or testing unknown substances. Let someone else do the police work. I quit.

But first, I had to finish with Jeremy.

Chapter 17

Ed's Story

After school, Ed was waiting for us by the front doors. He had our knapsacks slung over one shoulder and a bag of hockey equipment on the other. In his right hand was his hockey stick. In his left was a plastic bread bag which he held by the neck. He waved the bag in our direction.

"Come on," he yelled. "I've got lots of treats from the class party."

I hung back.

"Where are Davidson and Max?" I asked.

"They've gone. They said there was something they wanted to do before Aileen's party tonight."

Like what? Phone everyone in the neighbourhood to tell them what an idiot I was? Make a banner they could display in front of the school saying "Hunter Watson is a Loser"? There were lots of things they could be doing.

"Where's Jeremy?" Jason growled as he bounded down the school steps.

I peered all around to make sure no one was waiting to jump out at us before I joined them.

Ed shrugged our knapsacks off his shoulder, then held the bag open. Jason thrust his hand in, pulled out a broken cupcake and jammed it in his mouth.

"I don't know," Ed said. "He wasn't in class when I got back. And the bicycle slasher got away too. I followed him as far as the gym and then I lost him. I don't know which way he went . . . "

"It was Jeremy," Jason interrupted.

"What was?" Ed asked.

"The bicycle slasher," Jason said.

"Wow!" Ed said. "I didn't recognize him."

"It's his asthma," I said with a sigh. "I recognized the wheezing."

"Wow!" Ed said again. "That's amazing! Hiring you to be his detective and all the time it's him. That's really twisted!"

"So what are we going to do to him?" Jason asked.

"Go to the police," I said. I was filled with gloom. "Maybe they won't find out he hired me."

"Well, you did find out who the bicycle slasher was," Jason pointed out.

"Everyone else was just guessing. But you found out," Ed agreed.

"By accident," I said. "It makes a difference. He had me completely fooled. Everyone else seemed to know it all along."

"That's just Davidson and his big mouth," Ed said.

"What do you guys think about a science club?" I asked.

Ed groaned. Jason made a face.

"You're kidding, Hunter," he said. "That sounds like school."

"It's not really," I said. "We could make different chemicals.

Ed and Jason looked at each other and shook their heads.

"No, really," I said, "it'd be great. We could make explosions and stuff."

Ed's face cleared.

"That would be fun," he said.

"And invent different flavours and substances. You know, make our own chewing gum," I said to Jason.

He looked unconvinced.

"I like the detective club," he said.

"It was fun while it lasted," I agreed. "But something tells me we're not going to get much new business."

I was hoping one of them would disagree with

me. Instead Jason nodded and Ed just looked down at the bag in his hand.

"Have a cupcake," he said.

I took a mashed cupcake and stuffed it in my mouth. It didn't make me feel any better, but it didn't make me feel any worse, either. On a day like today, that seemed pretty good.

We wandered over to what would have been the scene of the crime and got my bike. Jason's bike rested against the fence a few feet away.

I looked around the playground. It was deserted. Everyone had rushed home to wait until it was time to go trick-or-treating.

"Where's your bike?" I asked Ed.

"Over there," he said, pointing across the playground.

"Why did you put it there?" I asked.

"I don't know," he mumbled.

"You must have had a reason," I said.

Jason wheeled his bike over to join us.

"Come on, Ed," he said. "You've been acting weird lately. What's going on?"

Ed turned a bright pink colour and shrugged his shoulders, dislodging his knapsack and dropping the hockey bag. He picked the knapsack up again and held it in his hands, staring at the buckle that held it shut. He looked as if he'd never seen a buckle before and was wondering how it worked.

"Jason's right, Ed," I said. "You've been acting very strange." I took a guess. "Jason thought you were in love."

Ed dropped the knapsack on his foot.

"Ouch!" he said.

"With Renner," I added.

Ed glared at Jason and then at me.

"Don't be stupid," he said. "Just because she talks to me all the time doesn't mean I'm in love with her." At the word "love" his voice curdled. "Mrs. Tweedie made me sit there, remember."

"Well, what about the note?" I asked.

"What note?" he said.

"That ridiculous note you wrote about me being in love with Aileen Goff."

"I didn't write that," he said.

I groaned. Hadn't I gotten anything right this week?

"Renner wrote it," he continued. "She grabbed my math test and wrote on the back of it."

"Why didn't you say so?" I shouted.

"I don't know," he said. He started fiddling with the buckle again.

"Of course you know," I said. "And why did you let me think something was going on with Renner?"

"Well," he said, looking in turn at the sky, his shoe and the buckle on his knapsack. "It was weird," he said and he took a quick look at me before gazing back up at the clouds.

I waited for a moment and pretended to examine the clouds myself. Jason sighed.

"I don't get it," he said.

I reconsidered all the evidence. Ed wasn't in love with Renner and he hadn't been attacking the bicycles. I thought about everything I'd heard and seen over the past week at school and the Saturday afternoon we'd dropped by his house.

"Is Simon okay?" I asked.

He looked at me with surprise.

"Simon's fine," he said. "He hates doing the cooking and he keeps shrivelling everything up in the microwave, but he's doing okay."

"Where's your mother?" I asked.

His face crumpled for a moment and he turned away from us but when he turned back, he looked calm and his voice was level.

"I don't know," he said. "But she's coming back. She phoned the school this afternoon to tell me she's coming to see me tomorrow at four and she wants me to be home."

"When did she go? What happened?" I asked.

"She left twelve days ago," Ed said, without hesitation. "She and my dad had a big fight."

Jason groaned.

"My parents are always fighting," he said.

"Not like this," Ed said. "I woke up in the middle of the night and she was crying. But I was too scared to go and see what was wrong. And in the morning when I got up, she was gone."

Now that he'd started talking, he didn't want to stop.

"My father said she'd be back by supper time and we weren't supposed to worry, but she wasn't back. And then by seven o'clock when she hadn't come back and she hadn't phoned, he took us out for a pizza and he told us that it didn't matter whether she came back or not because we could take perfectly good care of ourselves and we didn't need her anyway and we'd do such a good job we'd show her and he went on and on like that and then Simon started yelling at him about making her run away and by the time we left the restaurant, he wasn't speaking to Simon and Simon wasn't speaking to him and I couldn't think of anything to say because I was so shocked that she'd leave me. And I couldn't really think about anything else."

Jason looked worried.

"My parents don't fight like that," he said. "They just get noisy."

"So that's why there were all those pizza boxes," I said.

"Don't mention the word 'pizza' to me," Ed said. "I'm sick of pizza. And Chinese food."

"Do you want to come over to my place for supper?" I asked. "We're probably having chicken with broccoli and turnip or meatloaf and eggplant or something disgustingly healthy like that."

"Sure," Ed said. "That sounds great!"

"I'd rather have pizza," Jason said.

"At least it won't be brussels sprouts. We had them two nights ago," I said. "Even my mother wouldn't dare serve brussels sprouts twice in a single week."

"I like brussels sprouts," Ed said.

"I don't believe it," I said. "No one under the age of thirty-five likes brussels sprouts. It's against the law."

We pushed our bikes across the playground and waited while Ed unlocked his, hung his bag of hockey equipment from one handle and balanced his hockey stick across the handlebars. Then we set off for home, the sun momentarily gleaming from behind the torn clouds.

Chapter 18

Party Time

Ed and I had agreed to meet Jason at 8:00 at his house so we could walk together to Aileen's. No one wanted to look eager.

The wind had picked up again by then. It rattled the branches of the maple trees, snatching the few remaining clumps of yellow and red leaves and tossing them into the cold night air. Most of the trick-or-treaters were on their way home, their parents following, dragging bags stuffed with treats.

We went to Jason's and refuelled ourselves against the cold with leftover Halloween candy. By the time we got to Aileen's house, the streets were deserted.

We were among the last to arrive. Aileen's

mother and father answered the doorbell and escorted us to the family room.

"Hunter!" Aileen said, closing the door behind her parents. "We were going to call you." She and Julia left the group sitting in front of the tape deck and came to join us. Her skeleton earrings and pony-tail bounced in time to the music.

"Ed!" Renner shrieked from across the room. "I've saved you a place." She was sitting on the couch, watching a hockey game on the television. She had a bowl of popcorn in her lap.

Ed muttered something about checking out the score and wandered over to join her. Brent and Max were wrestling on the floor in front of the TV on a carpet of spilled popcorn.

Aileen saw me looking at them.

"They're so immature," she said, rolling her eyes. "But my mother made me invite everyone in the class."

"Even Jeremy?" I asked.

"Of course I knew he wouldn't come," she said. "And I phoned him this afternoon and told him not to."

"What did he say?" I asked.

"Nothing. What could he say!"

"Do you want to dance?" Julia asked Jason.

Jason took a step back and pretended to hide behind me.

"No way," he said.

Mrs. Goff opened the door and brought in a bowl of popcorn.

"We don't need any more popcorn," Aileen told her. "And please knock before you enter." Mrs. Goff ignored her, putting the popcorn between two other bowls on the table in front of the patio doors.

Aileen closed the family room door behind her.

"She's spying," she said darkly. "I'll bet you anything she's back in five minutes with another bowl of popcorn. Stop eating that!" she instructed Ed, who had already finished one bowl and was starting on another. "We'll never get rid of her if you keep eating."

Davidson Pruitt left the hockey game and sauntered over to join us.

"So you heard about Jeremy," I said.

He looked me up and down and nodded.

"Lucky you don't have to make your living doing this. You'd starve," he said and laughed.

"I was looking for proof," I said. "I was keeping an open mind and waiting for some solid evidence. You don't think the police would arrest someone just because we told them to."

"We had evidence," Davidson said. "That little kid saw him."

"Let's forget about it," I said. "I'm going to call the police tomorrow."

There was a knock at the door. Mr. Goff poked his head in.

"More popcorn?" he asked.

"Daddy!" Aileen screeched. "Go away!"

Mr. Goff pulled his head back in and closed the door.

Renner, who was balanced on the arm of the couch beside Ed, gave a little scream and fell into Ed's lap, knocking the bowl of popcorn onto the floor.

"I saw a face at the door," she said, pointing to the glass patio doors.

"Don't do that," Ed said. "You made me spill my popcorn." He got up to help himself to another bowl. I could hear the kernels crunching under his feet as he walked in front of the couch to the table by the doors.

"Get out of the way!" the hockey fans shouted. "We can't see."

"I don't know why they're watching hockey," Julia said to Jason. "Dancing is much more fun."

"I like hockey," Jason said.

"I sort of like it," Julia agreed. "Do you sort of like dancing?"

"I hate it," Jason said.

"Do you have any Coke?" Davidson asked Aileen. "That popcorn's made me thirsty."

"I'll get some," she said. She opened the family room door so quickly her mother almost fell into the room.

"We were just wondering if you wanted more

popcorn, dear," her mother asked.

"Coke," Aileen answered. "Everyone wants a Coke."

Her mother bustled off toward the kitchen. Aileen closed the door again.

Renner continued to wobble on the arm of the couch.

"Don't fall on top of me again," Ed said sternly.

I was looking at her, wondering if she was going to pay any attention to him, when I saw something flicker past the window. Something white. But as quickly as I saw it, it disappeared. I wandered over to the window and took a quick look around. Outside was a patio where two lawn chairs sat facing south. Several giant flowerpots filled with yellow flowers decorated the space.

"Don't you ever put the blinds down?" I asked Aileen.

"Not usually," she said. "Our backyard is fenced, so no one can see into the room."

"You've never had anyone hanging around the house staring inside, have you?" I asked.

"No," she said immediately. "Who'd want to do that?"

I shrugged.

There was a thumping sound on the family room door. Aileen opened it.

"For goodness sake, Aileen," her father said as he marched over to the table to put down a tray of soft-drink cans. "We were only gone for a minute. Don't keep closing the door."

She held the door open for him and closed it the moment he was gone.

Everyone clustered around the tray of soft drinks.

"Don't shake them up," Aileen yelled. "My parents will kill me if you get Coke on the carpet."

"I want Orange Crush," Max shouted.

Davidson threw him a can.

"Watch it, you almost hit me," Brent yelled.

Davidson threw him a can of Coke. As Brent reached up to catch it, I saw his face twist. As he lowered his right arm, his face relaxed.

That's interesting, I thought.

"Get me a Coke, will you?" Ed asked Renner, who jumped off her perch and pushed her way through to the table.

There was an explosive hissing sound and a fountain of orange drink sprayed into Brent's face as Max pulled the tab on his soft drink can.

"Stop that!" Aileen shrieked.

Brent howled that he would go blind. Max was lying on the floor, laughing. Aileen stalked over and grabbed the foaming can.

"You guys are pigs," she shrieked. She snatched Brent's unopened drink away, but he didn't notice. He was bent over double, shaking his head and rubbing his eyes with the front of his sweatshirt.

"I'm going to get you," he roared, reaching for Max, who rolled out of the way, catching Brent's right shoulder with the toe of his shoe.

Brent gasped and grabbed his shoulder.

"It was a joke," Max laughed. "Can't you take a joke?"

Brent rocked back and forth, his shoulder cradled in his left hand. His hair hung like weeds on his forehead and blotches of mucus and orange drink stained his sweatshirt. For once, both sides of his face matched. He was white with pain and rage.

Max was still giggling helplessly. Ed and Renner and the other people sitting on the couch and lounging in front of the television were smiling.

"Don't laugh at me," Brent roared, his voice thick and rattly. He cleared his throat. "That really hurt," he wheezed.

I stopped cold, my can of Coke halfway to my mouth. I finally understood. Jeremy wasn't the only person in our class who had asthma. Someone else did too. And that someone else was the bicycle slasher.

Chapter 19

Case Closed

"Why did you bash the bikes?" I asked Brent.

"What do you mean?" He spun to face me. "It was Jeremy. Everyone knows that." He cleared his throat again, but the tell-tale wheeze was still there.

"I didn't know you had asthma," I said, keeping my voice steady.

"I used to," he said and coughed. "I don't any more."

The room was quiet. The hockey commentator announced a penalty, but no-one was watching the game.

"Sounds like it's come back," I said.

Brent cleared his throat again and glared at me.

"I have a cold," he said.

Again a shape drifted past the patio doors. Someone or something was out there, in the black wind, watching. I decided to try a different approach.

"How's your shoulder?" I asked.

"What?" Brent said. He glanced at his hand clutching his shoulder, then looked back to me. "It really hurts. But that's because Max, the creep," he hissed at Max, "kicked it."

"Do you think it's bruised?" I asked.

"I don't know," he said in a puzzled voice.

"Let's see," I said calmly.

He looked around the room. I could see him wondering what I was up to. He shrugged and pulled the black sweatshirt down over his shoulder. A deep purple bruise stained the pale skin.

"Yeah, it's bruised all right," I said.

Brent's voice thickened. "So what?" he growled, tugging the sweatshirt back up over his shoulder. "Max really belted me."

Someone agreed with him. Everyone else remained silent.

I slowly shook my head and spoke in my coldest voice.

"He nudged you," I said. "It was just a tap, that's all. The reason it hurt so much is because you'd rammed it once already, earlier today."

I could see by his expression that he still didn't understand.

"When you ran back into the school, after trying to stab my bike. Ed almost caught you, didn't he, because instead of opening the doors to the school, you were going so fast you ran right into them. Shoulder first."

When I got to the part about Ed almost catching him, I saw Brent's eyes gleam. His left lip curled in a smile.

"Prove it," he taunted. "I could have got that bruise from Max."

"Any dummy knows that it takes several hours for a bruise to show," I sneered. I didn't want to give him room to think. I had to keep attacking. "It's not like a cut. Of course, you'd know all about cuts, wouldn't you? A couple of quick jabs with a knife is all it takes to wreck a bike. Doesn't matter whose bike it is. You didn't even realize you were cutting up Jeremy's bike. You were just destroying every bike that you saw that was better than yours. And you were too stupid to know that sooner or later we'd catch up with you."

"I'm not stupid," Brent snarled.

"You think it's smart to go around busting people's bikes? I think you're stupid. You've always been stupid. You . . . "

"No, I think it's fun," he howled. From under the left sleeve of his sweatshirt, he pulled out the pocket knife I'd seen once before and clutched it like a dagger. "I think it's lots of fun watching you guys sweat. You think you've got everything, don't you? Well, look what happens to those fancy new bikes of yours." He stabbed the air with the gleaming knife, his face twisted. "What do you think of those great bikes now?" Again, the knife slashed through the space between us.

I had hoped he'd talk himself out of his rage so I could grab the knife away. Instead, his anger was building.

Everyone sat frozen in shock, their eyes held by the shining blade. I sent mental messages to Mr. and Mrs. Goff, urging them to open the door and ask us if we wanted more popcorn. Renner buried her face in Ed's shoulder. He didn't seem to notice, but stared at Brent, his mouth open.

"Okay, okay," I said, breaking into Brent's bitter flow. "Let's cool it."

"Don't you tell me what to do," Brent screamed.

A white face pressed itself against the window behind him and waved at me.

Aileen gasped.

My heart lurched in my chest, but then I recognized the pale figure. I tried to signal Jeremy by waving back at him, waving him around to the front of the house to alert Mr. and Mrs. Goff. At the same time, there was a knock on the family room door.

"Daddy!" Aileen screamed and ran toward it.

In a single motion, Brent leaped over the table and slipped through the patio doors into the back yard. We charged out after him, ready to give chase.

But it was unnecessary. He was lying in a huddle a few metres from the doors, moaning and hugging his knee. Beside him was a shattered clay pot. Dark earth and yellow flowers spilled onto the patio stones.

Jeremy was standing guard above him.

"He tripped on his shoelace and fell over the big flowerpot," Jeremy said to me. "Do you think he broke anything?"

"Only the flowerpot," I said.

Jeremy's round face was pale in the moonlight.

"I came to apologize for running out on you this afternoon," he said. "I was sitting in class when I suddenly remembered I hadn't changed the water in Spike's tank. I didn't want to lose him too, so I just got up and headed for home. Luckily I was in time. But after I changed his water and checked everything, I realized I'd walked out on you. I knew Aileen didn't want me at her party, so I was hanging around . . . "

"Did you hear what Brent said?" I interrupted him.

"Yeah. I wondered if it might be him," Jeremy said.

"What!" I was thunderstruck.

"I saw him going through the Lost and Found box the afternoon Max's bike was busted. I didn't think about it at the time, but later I realized that he might have found a red jacket in there."

"Why didn't you tell me?" I shouted.

"I was worried about Drifter," he said. "He wasn't swimming properly. I forgot about Brent."

Maybe a nuclear bomb would distract Jeremy from his fish. Maybe not.

Mr. and Mrs. Goff shooed us back inside, where we waited for the police and Brent's parents to appear. By that time it was clear that the party was over. Ed was down to the final kernels in the last bowl of popcorn when Jason came over to thump me on the back .

"We're in business again!" he said happily.

I spoke a few words with Max, who thanked me for catching Brent, said my thank-yous to Aileen and her mother — her father was on his hands and knees sponging the family room carpet — grabbed Jason and Ed and made my way home, tired but content. The case was closed.

* * *

Brent didn't come back to school after the Halloween party show-down. Some people said he was grounded; Renner was sure he'd been sent to jail. In the end, I uncovered the truth.

It wasn't easy. I found a witness to a meeting

between Mrs. Boswell and Brent's parents. Unfortunately that witness was Shane Brewster, a grade four boy who had been trying out some new swear words one afternoon recess when Mr. Feeney was on yard duty. Shane was sent to sit on one of the straight-back chairs outside the principal's office until she was ready to talk to him.

The office door was open, but he wasn't listening to the conversation. It was just a bunch of adults blabbing away, he told me. It wasn't until he heard the man mention Brent's name that my eavesdropper pricked up his ears.

"He was angry, Hunter," Shane told me later. "Angry at the school and at Mrs. Boswell, but angry with Brent, too. Mrs. Wexler wasn't angry, she just kept saying how sorry they were. Brent had been causing trouble at home, but they didn't know he was causing trouble anywhere else. She was talking about some doctor they were taking Brent to see when Mrs. Boswell caught me peeking into her office. She slammed the door right in my face and, Hunter, you should have heard what she said to me later. I got a detention from now until next month!"

I thanked Shane for his help, and told him I hoped the month's detention passed quickly.

"No problem," he said, grinning. "I bring a deck of cards with me to detention and play for quarters with anyone else who gets sent to the office. So far

I've won $11.75! Want to have a game?"

I told him I didn't have time for games and left. I made a mental note to check any deck of cards he might use before agreeing to any games. That kind of winning streak sounded too good to be true.

Jason gave me the next clue. He was jogging down Brent's street one Friday morning, late for school as usual, when he saw Brent and his father getting into their car.

"I almost didn't recognize him, Hunter," Jason told me in a shocked voice. "He was wearing grey trousers and a green suit jacket." He sniffed and scrubbed his nose on the sleeve of his sweatshirt. "Brent even wore a striped tie. It was terrible!"

From his description of Brent's clothing, I deduced that Brent was being sent to a private boys' school north of the city, one that had a reputation for straightening out "problem" kids.

Surprisingly enough, Aileen found out the rest. Her parents called the Wexlers to find out how Brent was. They were told that the whole family was getting counselling and they felt they now understood Brent's problem. Maybe, we thought, everything would be okay.

So life returned to normal. Jeremy had saved the remaining neon tetras, Aileen had a new bike. Max's mother promised to buy him a new bike in the spring, when the sales started. Davidson's father still had a wallet full of credit cards and Ed's mom was home, for the time being at least.

"Class!" Mrs. Tweedie shouted above the noise of scraping chairs and snatches of conversation. "Class, I have an exciting announcement to make."

After all that had happened, it was hard to imagine there was anything exciting left in the world. But Mrs. Tweedie looked so pink and happy, her face glowing, that I stopped stuffing books into my backpack and listened.

"I'd like you to know that I'll be leaving this class as of mid-April and you'll have a supply teacher for the remainder of the year."

There was a chorus of groans.

"I hate supply teachers," Renner told Ed.

"Why are you going, Mrs. Tweedie?" Julia asked.

"I'm taking maternity leave," Mrs. Tweedie said, smoothing the front of her skirt. "I'm having a baby."

The girls cheered. Some of the boys whistled.

"How much do you want to bet it's a boy?" Davidson asked Max.

Mrs. Tweedie broke into the noise. "And I want to apologize if the class hasn't run as smoothly as it should," she said. "I've been feeling sick and also worried because I was having some problems. But everything's better now. I'm fine. The doctor tells me the baby's fine. I'm going to miss you."

There was an eruption of noise. Davidson was

taking bets on the baby's sex, Aileen and Julia were collecting names for it. I don't think many people heard Mrs. Tweedie promise to come back next year.

A crumpled ball of paper flew across the room, hitting me on the side of the head. As I smoothed it open, I noticed that on one side was someone's scribbled French dictation. The other side said, "Hunter Watson loves blueberry upside-down cake. My mom baked some for us yesterday." The note was unsigned. I scrunched it up into a ball and threw it as hard as I could at Ed's back. He turned and grinned.

We left together.

About the Author

Ann Aveling has always been a mystery lover. When her kids Lucy, Nick and Paula came along, she read mysteries to them too. But after reading hundreds of sleuth stories, Ann found that she could solve even the most difficult ones in a snap. In order to make mysteries fun again, she started to write her own.

Her writing headquarters is her home in Toronto, which she shares with her kids and her husband, Roger. Ann is also a teacher, and enjoys gardening and sports in her free time.